THE MAN I THOUGHT I KNEW

TWO-FACED #1

E. L. TODD

HARTWICK PUBLISHING

Hartwick Publishing

The Man I Thought I Knew

Copyright © 2020 by E. L. Todd

All rights reserved.

No part of this book may be reproduced in any form or by any electronic or mechanical means, including information storage and retrieval systems, without written permission from the author, except for the use of brief quotations in a book review.

CONTENTS

1.	Carson	1
2.	Carson	11
3.	Carson	25
4.	Carson	39
5.	Carson	49
6.	Carson	57
7.	Charlie	69
8.	Carson	75
9.	Carson	89
10.	Charlie	107
11.	Carson	115
12.	Charlie	129
13.	Carson	143
14.	Carson	151
15.	Carson	173
16.	Carson	181
17.	Carson	193
18.	Charlie	203
19.	Carson	213
20.	Carson	229
21.	Dax	253
22.	Dax	273
23.	Carson	281
24.	Carson	295
	Also by E. L. Todd	311

ONE
CARSON

I knocked on the open door. "You wanted to see me, boss?"

His glasses sat on the bridge of his nose as he looked down at the paper in his hands. With salt-and-pepper hair and a matching beard, he was one of those handsome men who aged nicely, like a fine wine that only got better with time. Without looking up, he waved me in with his fingers.

The office was busy with people making copies, talking on the phone at their cubicles, occasionally yelling across the room at one another for something. It was casual, somewhat chaotic, like the floor of the stock exchange.

We were the most respected newspaper in the world, so we had to hustle and make every second count. Sometimes shouting at a neighbor was easier than a stupid email that ended with "Sincerely Yours."

I stepped into the office and took a seat, knowing he'd called me in there to hand me the next assignment. My heart always raced during these moments, because I worked my ass off for the good stories, and every time I was given one, I assumed that my last article had been well received.

He finally put down the paper and took off his glasses to regard me. "Carson, I've been given a few leads from anonymous sources. The information checks out. It's yours if you want it—"

"Absolutely."

He held up his hand to silence me before I ran my mouth and said a million things. "I haven't even told you what it is yet."

"You know I never turn down a story."

"But this dangerous. You gotta keep your head down, Carson."

"Psh." I flipped my hair over my shoulder. "I can handle Baghdad, so I can handle this."

His hard, beady eyes stayed on me, slightly annoyed. "The big banks are discriminating against their clients. They're only handing out large loans to the clients that have at least a hundred million dollars in their accounts. Businesses that actually need it are either being denied, or their paperwork is getting lost. My sources say there's a bigger scheme going on here, that investors are pulling some kind of strings to make their pockets fuller. Sources suspect corporations are inflating their net worth with these loans, to attract more investors. Might be the biggest case of corporate fraud we've ever seen. You're gonna have to ask questions people don't want to be asked—and you might pay for it."

I wasn't scared of anything—especially suits. "I got this."

He regarded me for another moment before he handed me the folder. "Be safe, Carson. I don't want your body to be found in the Hudson."

I opened it and took a look inside. "Corporate fraud...so easy." I rose to my feet and gave him a thumbs-up. "Thanks so much, Vince." I turned to leave his office.

"Carson."

I turned back around in the doorway.

"You're one of the best journalists I've got. You don't need to keep proving yourself."

I hustled like any day might be my last. A fire had been lit under my ass, and work had become my entire life. I wanted my name to mean something, to command respect in the journalistic community. "You know I've got an ass that don't quit."

AT THE END of the day, I stopped by Charlie's cubicle. "Ready?"

Without acknowledging me, he logged out of his computer, took his flash drive, and then packed his bag to leave. He walked beside me, and we left the floor together, waiting until we were in the elevator with the doors closed.

"What story did Vince give you?" Charlie was in a long-sleeved shirt and jeans, nearly a foot taller than me, having kind eyes that matched his kind heart underneath that strong chest.

"The story of the century."

"Start talking."

"Corporate fraud. The banks are in cahoots with the biggest corporations in the country, using their loans to inflate their stock values."

Charlie had to blink a few times to process what I'd said. It was unbelievable, to me as well as to him. It was definitely the story of the century. "You've got to be joking."

"I don't have the details, but that's what we know from sources."

"Jesus Christ..."

"Yep." The elevator lowered to the bottom floor, and I took advantage of the opportunity to dance around, raise my hands over my head, shake my ass in celebration. "Who's the baddest bitch in this place?"

He gripped the strap of his satchel and chuckled. "Carson, this could be dangerous."

"Dangerous is my middle name." I kept dancing.

"I'm serious."

"Look, it's always dangerous. I wouldn't like my job if it weren't."

"I would." He shook his head.

"And Vince asked me. Mwah." I shook my shoulders to make my tits shake. "He could have asked Arthur or Cameron, but nope—he asked me." I cupped my mouth and shouted in the elevator. "Who's the hottest bitch in this place?"

He chuckled. "Congrats, Carson."

"Come on." I nudged him in the side, still dancing.

He rolled his eyes before he started to dance, moving in the silence to the gears of the elevator. We made our own music together, spinning around, shaking our hips, partying without a single sound.

Then the doors opened on the lobby.

We immediately straightened, seeing people waiting to get inside.

"Hey, how you doing?" I strutted past them.

"Have a good one," Charlie said, moving with me to get past the crowd.

We walked away together, suppressing the grins on our faces.

"Was that the owner of the paper?" Charlie asked.

"Yep." I burst out laughing.

He laughed too. "Fuck."

CHARLIE AND I WERE ROOMMATES. It was the only way we could afford to live in Manhattan, which was a much better commute than taking two trains from Brooklyn. It was a two-bedroom apartment with a good-sized living room but didn't have much of a kitchen.

But it was perfect for us.

"What do you want for dinner?" I stared into the fridge, my hand gripping the handle on the outside.

Charlie fell onto the couch, putting his feet on the table. "Beer."

"Well, we don't have that."

"We're out?" He dropped his head back and sighed. "Goddammit."

"We can have some delivered…for a small fortune."

"Maybe next time I get a raise."

"So, we can make—"

A knock sounded on the door.

Charlie was closer, so he yelled, "It's open!"

Denise walked inside, her purse strap across her chest so her bag could rest on her opposite hip. She had short blond hair, a little more height than me, and she had blue eyes, unlike mine. "Hey. What's for dinner?"

Charlie shifted on the couch so he could look at her. "Beer. But we realized we're out."

"Oh…then I should just go." She turned back to the door and chuckled. "Nah, I'm kidding. I still want to see my little sister even when there's no beer or food."

I shut the fridge and sighed. "We're gonna have to order something. I've been so swamped at work I haven't had time to go to the store." I came back into the living room to face her.

"You guys want to get Thai food?" Denise turned to Charlie. "There's that great place just across the street."

Charlie rose to his feet and joined us behind the couch. "I'm not going to say no to that." He slid his hands into his pockets and looked at her, his eyes focused for a few seconds too long. "You in, Carson?"

"It's better than starving, so let's do it." I grabbed my purse, and we headed across the street. We got a table, and I ordered a Thai iced tea. "What's new, Denise?"

She shrugged. "Just work, work, work. What about you?"

Charlie sat beside her, his eyes on her most of the time, even though I was directly across from her. "Carson got the article of a lifetime."

"Really?" she asked, turning back to me. "I feel like you've already gotten three of those."

I shrugged. "I'm just so good that it keeps happening."

She chuckled but rolled her eyes. "What is it?"

"Corporate fraud."

"Doesn't require travel, right?" Denise asked. "Because we'll miss you too much."

"Not sure," I said. "I just got the assignment like two hours ago, but I'm eager to get started."

We ordered our food and then made small talk, chatting about the next game night, the creepy dude at the gym who sweated on everything, and the wait for summer to hit the city. Charlie was quiet, like he usually was around Denise. He kept his head down and ate most of the time.

"So, when are we going to get together?" Denise asked. "Since you've been so busy lately."

"How about Saturday?" I asked. "We'll either have a game night or go bowling."

"Going to bring Boy Toy?" Denise teased.

I shrugged. "Maybe. Depends on if I'm horny or not."

"Well, Boy Toy is pretty hot," Denise said. "Don't see it going anywhere?"

I shook my head quickly. "I don't want it to go anywhere, and he knows that. Guys have their regulars on the side. Why can't I have mine?"

"Very true." Denise finished the rest of her tea before she stood up. "I'm gonna powder my nose, and then we'll go." She left her satchel behind and walked off.

I put my leftovers in the paper bag the waitress had left on the table.

Charlie was right by the window, so he looked outside, his elbows on the table. He had dirty-blond hair, bright eyes, and a muscular physique. He was a few years older than me, but he shared my immaturity.

"You need to stop making it so obvious."

His eyes shifted back to mine, his expression defensive right away.

"One, stop staring. Two, don't be so quiet."

He drank his tea and ignored what I'd said.

"I'm just trying to help you."

"Got it." He sat back in the chair and rubbed the back of his neck.

I'd known Charlie since we started working together at the *New York Press*, and he had no problem getting dates, picking up women at bars and the gym, but Denise had always been under his skin and wouldn't go away...for years. "I'm sorry."

He shrugged. "It is what it is."

TWO
CARSON

I sat across from Jerry Hempstead in the booth, wearing a black cocktail dress and heels, my glass of Bordeaux in front of me. "Your corporation brought in more than a billion dollars last year. That's a *B*. Not an *M*. And yet, you accepted this loan from the bank when you shouldn't even need the funds. Let's talk about that." I picked up my glass and took a drink, my lipstick smearing on the edge.

Jerry was a middle-aged man who had a crooked look about him. He was a cliché, looking as evil as he probably was. He'd been there picking up a prostitute when I'd intervened, embarrassing him in front of his tail and cornering him in this booth. Now, I had dirt on him—which was why he was still sitting there.

Overweight and sweaty despite the cold temperature in the bar, he stared at me with a ferocious glare. "Not much to say."

"According to my records, you just raised the value of your company by five points a week ago, at the same time this loan closed. You want to talk about that?"

He gave me a grin, but it wasn't kind or warm. It was more of a sneer. "Sweetheart, you talk the talk. You probably walk the walk. But you have no idea what you're getting into. I suggest you let it go."

"Nah." I took another drink. "I never let anything go. This problem won't go away. Every time you're out trying to pick up a piece of ass while your wife is out of town with the kids, I'll be there."

"Will you be the piece of ass?"

"Oh honey, you couldn't afford me."

"I disagree. I have something you want. You want some information, it's gonna cost you." He nodded to the doorway. "Get on those skinny knees and blow me good, and maybe I'll give you a few names." He was sleazy, disgusting, and the criminal I accused him of being.

"Nah, I'm good." I pulled out the recorder and set it on the table. "Work with me, Jerry. I have a good relationship with the Feds so I can get you immunity if you make this worthwhile."

He glanced at the recorder before he flicked it away, making it slide off the table and back onto my seat. "Do you know how to swim?"

My eyes narrowed on his face, knowing he was going to say something sinister in a few seconds.

"Because you're gonna be dropped in the middle of the ocean if you keep asking these questions." He grabbed my glass, took a drink and got his spit on the edge, and then scooted out of the booth. "Have a good one, Carson."

I didn't look at him as he walked away. "Give my best to the missus..." I sat perfectly straight, my empty glass full of his spit in front of me. Now I needed another drink, a stronger one.

It was a quiet night in the bar, probably because it was the middle of the week and summer was still a few weeks away. When the hot season arrived, there'd be so many tourists they'd be breathing down your neck in every hot spot in Manhattan.

I needed some quotes for this story, but that was impossible if nobody would talk. I had bank documents and recordings of private conversations, but I needed a little more to actually break this story. I'd contacted my source at the FBI, but I wasn't getting a callback.

Distracted by my thoughts, I didn't notice the man approach my table. He placed a glass of Bordeaux in front of me, replacing the defiled one that sleazy man had ruined. The man helped himself to the seat across from me.

"Look, I'm really not in the..." I shut my mouth when I got a look at the guy. His sleeves were rolled to his elbows, his forearms chiseled and covered with those corded veins I liked. He had tanned skin, like he was an outdoorsy kind of man, and his broad shoulders showed a commitment to the gym. His arms were thick, and he was ripped, maximizing the muscle without being bulky. He was muscular but lean, like he lifted weights and was a runner. But his face was the best part. He had that cut jawline sprinkled with dark stubble, dark eyes, and short dark hair. His neck had a few corded veins running down underneath the neckline of his long-sleeved shirt.

And he had a glass of scotch in his hand.

No beer. No wine. Just straight liquor.

Wow, this guy was something.

He lifted the glass slightly, swirled the amber liquid a bit, and then brought it to his lips for a quick drink. He licked his lips before he set it down again, looking at me like he'd already said hello even though he hadn't said a word.

It was rare for me to be caught off guard by a man, to be thoroughly impressed by just his energy and appearance. But he made my mouth close, made me stare, made me a little nervous.

After another sip, he spoke. "I thought you deserved a drink after you handled that asshole."

I didn't even care that he'd been eavesdropping. "A couple drinks, actually." I took a drink, letting what was left of my lipstick smear against the glass. "And thank you." I held up my glass before I set it down again.

He nodded.

"Oh no...you're the strong and silent type."

He tilted his head slightly, his eyes narrowing.

"I'm a sucker for the strong and silent type."

His eyes looked out the window for a second, a small smile moving onto his lips. He turned back to his scotch and took a drink, like the booze didn't affect him at all. "I was about to head home when I overheard your conversation. Never heard a woman handle herself like that."

"Then you need to get out more."

He grinned again, and it was such a handsome look on him, a soft touch to all his hardness. The shadow on his jawline was so masculine and sexy, and the deep brown color of his eyes made him look dangerous, even when he smiled. He leaned against the back of the leather booth, his shoulders wide, his long arms reaching the table where his hands cupped his glass. "Are you a cop?"

"No," I said with a laugh. "I'm a journalist."

"Why is that a funny question?"

"Because I don't have the spine for a job like that."

"After what I heard, I disagree." He leaned forward, his elbows landing on the table, his palm circling over the top of his glass, his fingers along the edge. "What kind of journalist are you?"

"I write for the *New York Press*."

His eyebrows rose, like he was familiar with the paper and its prestige. "That's impressive."

I appreciated the compliment, but I didn't respond to it. My success usually intimidated men, along with my loud mouth and opinionated comments. But so far, he didn't seem like one of those guys.

"It seems a bit dangerous, based on what I heard."

"Oh, that was nothing." I took another drink, glad that the wine had settled in my stomach and made me relax a bit. This man set all my nerves on fire. My conversations with Jerry got me nowhere, but it was worth it...because it led to this.

"He basically threatened to kill you."

I rolled my eyes. "I'm like a cat. I have nine lives."

"And what life are you on now?"

I thought of all my close calls, all the assignments that were too dangerous for people to take. "Probably five."

"Then you're running out."

"Eh." I shrugged. "We gotta die sometime, right?"

He swirled his glass again before he took a drink. Then it was empty, and he pushed the glass to the edge of the table, as if he knew it would get the attention of the busty bartender.

It did. She came right away and refilled his glass.

"Thanks." He pulled it back to him and took another drink.

Damn, this man could drink.

"What was your most dangerous assignment?"

"Iraq."

His eyebrows rose again, slightly.

"ISIS."

"You went alone?"

"It's actually easier to travel alone than in a group. Draws less attention."

He stared at me, that focused stare, like he had no problem with intimacy, like he was so confident that silence only strengthened him, not weakened him. Without saying a word, he expressed his opinion, found me respectable rather than crazy. "How long were you there?"

"About four weeks."

"That's a long time."

"When it comes to complex situations like that, it takes time to really understand the problem, to get people to trust you enough to talk, to share information with you that could get them beheaded. I'm usually working on multiple stories at a time, so I also utilized that stint to discuss life for the women there, the sexism and prejudice they face on a regular basis."

"And the danger doesn't scare you?"

I shook my head before I took a drink. "I can handle myself."

He looked into the contents of his glass, a slight smile on his lips. "I believe it."

It was surprising how many men chose to give me a lecture about my profession, especially when I never asked. They warned me about the dangers, that it was no place for a woman, that I should stick to the lifestyle section of the paper—even though there wasn't one. "So, why is a hunk like you sitting alone in a bar?" Guys like this didn't grow on trees. When they did exist, they were usually so arrogant and stupid that a simple conversation with them was painful. But this guy seemed to have the looks...and the brains.

"My date canceled."

"This must be a blind date, then. Because if she knew what you looked like..." I shook my head. "That bitch definitely wouldn't cancel."

A slight smile spread his lips. "No, we know each other."

I appreciated the fact that he didn't lie, that he didn't just say whatever I wanted to hear to get into my pants. A man like him probably had regulars on top of regulars. There was never a lonely night. If he wanted someone, he could just send a text, and she'd show up at his door in a few minutes, like hot pizza delivery.

I would love to be one of his regulars.

"But I'm glad she canceled."

I tried to suppress my grin by drinking from my wineglass, not letting that comment get under my skin. But he was smooth, and after I licked my lips, I smiled.

"I never would have met such a badass woman."

"Badass, huh? I think most people would just call me a bitch."

"Sometimes I wonder if they're the same thing." He took a deep drink then licked his lips.

I liked that comment—a lot. "You want to go out Saturday night?" I had no problem asking a guy out. If I waited until the end of the night, it was guaranteed he would make a pass at me. But I never liked to wait for things to happen to me. I chose to *happen* to things.

He didn't smile, but his eyes lit up a bit. "I'd love to."

I pulled out my phone then stared at him.

He smiled then told me his number.

I wrote it down and quickly typed Boy Toy #2 under his name. Then I put my phone back into my clutch. "I'll see you then." I grabbed the glass and finished the rest of my wine. "And thank you for the wine."

He didn't ask why I was leaving or where I was going. He watched me scoot out of the booth and stand. "Dax."

"Carson."

He got to his feet then extended his hand to me.

I took it, giving him a firm shake. "*Really* nice to meet you, Dax."

He squeezed my wrist gently before he let me go. "The pleasure is mine, Carson."

"OH MY GOD. Shut up and listen to me." I walked through the door and tossed my clutch on the entryway table.

Charlie stilled at the round dining table, his notes scattered around him next to his laptop. He looked up, bewildered by the comment. "Done and done."

I sat in the chair across from him and slipped off my pumps, my feet screaming from the long walk from the bar to our apartment. "I met the most gorgeous man I've ever seen. He's got dark eyes, which I love, and this sexy stubble on his jaw." I dragged my fingers across my jawline, where his hair would be. "He's got dark hair too. You know, dark and dangerous kind of vibe. And he's the strong and silent type. Doesn't say much. Damn. Sooooo sexy."

Charlie stared at me blankly. "Then why are you home right now?"

"Come on, I'm not gonna go home with him right away."

He raised an eyebrow. "Because...?"

"Because I want him to think about me for a bit. That way, when it does happen, it'll be super hot. You know, I'll send him texts of me in my lingerie, make him look forward to it. He'll be like a bronco coming out of the chute."

"When are you seeing him?"

"Saturday."

"You're bringing him along, then?"

"Yep."

"What about Boy Toy #1?"

"What about him?" I asked. "He sees other people, and so do I."

"But I thought you liked him."

"I do." I was playing the field and loving every second of it. I liked having a man to call when I needed some companionship. Men had regulars all the time, so why couldn't I? Dax probably had a message box full of admirers. Why couldn't I have the same? I never led anyone on. My complete detachment was clear.

"So...are we going to talk about what you actually went out for?"

"Oh shit." I smacked my forehead playfully. "Of course. Well, Jerry is a big sleazebag—"

"Guys who commit corporate fraud tend to be."

"He was picking up a whore when I intervened. I tried to grind him down, but he wouldn't talk. Told me to mind my own business if I didn't want to end up in an oil drum."

"And that doesn't concern you?" he asked with a raised eyebrow.

"You know how many times I've been threatened like that?" I started counting on both hands. "Like a hundred times. And I'm still here."

He shook his head slightly. "So, he wouldn't go on record?"

"Nope. Douchebag."

"Can't blame him for not incriminating himself."

"But he seems to think they might get away with it, even though they're being investigated. Getting those fancy lawyers won't save his ass."

"Those fancy lawyers save most asses."

"Well, my article will rip them all to shreds."

"And probably have no real consequence, because the bad guys always get away with everything."

It was depressing to think about, but it wouldn't change my integrity. My articles made a difference, changed the world, broke the news people least expected. I'd had articles that launched investigations from the CIA and the FBI. "This article will be different."

"Hope so. Did you tell Vince?"

I nodded. "I sent him a text. He didn't respond." I relaxed into the chair and crossed my legs. "Have you bagged any dates lately?"

"I'm still seeing Jennifer from the gym, but it's not going anywhere."

I pitied Charlie because he was in a complicated situation—and there was nothing he could do about it. "You know, I could always move out..." Charlie was my closest friend, and I loved living with him. Our personalities were compatible, and we balanced each other out. Some people thought it was strange to have a guy roommate and assumed we hooked up all the time, but there was no attraction between us. "Move in with Denise or something."

He shook his head. "It's okay, Carson."

"I just don't think it's ever going to get better. Maybe some space will be good."

He shook his head again. "Carson, you're my person. I don't want to sacrifice this friendship for anything."

I grinned. "I thought Matt was your person?"

He chuckled. "He's my best friend, but I can't talk to him the way I talk to you."

"Because I'm a woman?"

"No. You just understand me better. I tell you things without getting judgment in return. We work together, so I have someone to talk about those things with. I'm not sure what I'm going to do, but I don't want you to move out."

I leaned over the table and smiled at him. "You love me."

He rolled his eyes.

"Come on, admit it."

"I'd rather die."

"Oh, shut up." I swatted his hand where it rested on the table. "I'm your bestie."

"Matt is technically my bestie—"

"But if you can't say that to his face, then it doesn't count."

He sighed in defeat. "Fine... I love you."

I grinned wide, with a hint of victory. "I love you too, Charlie." I blew him a kiss.

He brushed it away with his hand.

I chuckled at his rejection. "Looks like we're roommates forever."

"I hope not. I was hoping to get a raise or promotion at some point."

"Yeah, that's never going to happen." There just wasn't enough money in publishing. People wanted free content, so no one bought newspapers anymore. If this were fifteen years ago, I'd be making a phenomenal salary, but now I made just enough to live in the city. But I'd never been in this for the money, so it wasn't an issue. I would probably have a roommate for the rest of my life. "But we're going to be together forever, so it's fine."

"I do want a wife and kids at some point."

"That's fine. I can just live with you guys."

He chuckled. "That would happen, wouldn't it?"

"Yeah, because whoever you marry is gonna be an awesome chick, so we'll be best friends, naturally, and she'll never want me to leave. Plus, free babysitting."

"And what about when you get married?"

I continued to plaster the smile on my face, but it was forced. I didn't feel it in my heart where it belonged. "I'm too wild to settle down. With all the travel required for my job, the late hours, and the alleyway meetings...it's not for me. Plus, you know how many hot guys I'm gonna meet?"

Charlie watched me with a stern expression, but his eyes slowly turned apologetic, like he didn't believe a word I said but chose to let it go. "Yeah...a ton."

THREE
CARSON

Kat stood beside me at the high-top table, her untouched cosmo in front of her. She kept glancing at Charlie and Matt at the bar, her long dark hair pulled over one shoulder. "So, where's this guy?"

"I don't know. I told him to meet me here thirty minutes ago. I've sent him lots of dirty pictures throughout the week, so he'll definitely show."

"Ooh, let me see."

I pulled out my phone and showed her the pictures, wearing a bodysuit in one, a baby doll in the other.

"Damn, girl. You look hawt." She scrolled through the pictures. "He'll definitely show up. No doubt about it. He's totally jerked off to these, by the way."

"I'm waiting for the real thing."

Both Kat and I snapped our heads in his direction, seeing him standing at the table beside us, drink in hand, looking sexy as hell in a black t-shirt and jeans. He gave us a slight smile as he regarded us.

Kat dropped the phone onto the table, where it made a loud clank. Then she turned to me and whispered, "You weren't kidding...he's super hot."

"Girl, if I say a man is hot, he's hawt," I whispered back.

His eyes shifted back and forth between us as he could hear every word. He grinned slightly, like he was amused by it.

"I'm gonna excuse myself to the restroom to give you a second to chat," Kat said. "But ask if he has any hawt friends." She gave my side a gentle pinch before she turned to him and shook his hand. "Kat. Lovely to meet you." She winked then headed to the restroom with her clutch under her arm.

Now that she was gone, he moved closer to me, a scotch in hand. "I've got a few guys."

"Ooh...perfect." I held my cosmo as I came close to him, my hand sliding over his forearm casually, lightly giving him affection without overdoing it.

His eyes moved down to my body, looking at my figure in my tight dress. He wasn't discreet about it because he didn't want his intentions to be discreet. He pivoted his body toward me, pulling his arm away from my touch and placing it on my hips, bringing us closer together so our mouths were close.

Jesus Christ, he was so hot.

His stubble was gone because he'd shaved, but it showed off his rugged chin, his sexy lips. His brown eyes were deep and complex, like he had a million thoughts going through his brain at once. His hand was large against my body, with long fingers and webs of veins all over the top. "It's been a long week."

"Yeah?"

"Torturing me with those photos."

"Torture?" My fingers immediately moved to his chin, feeling the softness now that the coarse hair had been removed. My thumb swiped across his bottom lip, wanting to feel his gorgeous features with my bare fingertips. "Honey, you ain't seen nothing yet..."

His eyes darkened slightly, the change of expression so subtle it was easy to miss. But it was obvious to me, sexy to me. He could convey so much with just his looks, his sexy, brooding lips.

Matt and Charlie came back to the table with their drinks.

"Damn, that was fast." Matt set his beer on the table. "Leave the woman alone for a minute, and a new man is up to bat."

I kept my eyes on Dax, my fingers moving down his neck to his chest—his rock-hard chest. "This is the super-sexy guy I was telling you about." I turned away and looked at Charlie. "Dax, this is Charlie, my bestie."

"Hey." Charlie moved his hand over the table to Dax.

Dax took it and shook.

"Wait, bestie?" Matt asked, looking at Charlie. "I thought I was your bestie?"

Charlie rolled his eyes. "You're a guy. You can't be my bestie."

"But I'm gay," he snapped. "I'm totally qualified."

I snapped my fingers repeatedly. "Matt, focus. This is Dax."

"Sorry." Matt shook his hand. "And you're right, he's gorgeous." He winked at Dax.

Instead of being uncomfortable, Dax grinned. "Thanks."

"You got any gay bros with you?" Matt asked.

Dax shook his head. "Unfortunately, no."

"Damn." Matt took a drink of his beer.

Charlie looked past me. "Denise is here."

"Ooh." I looked past Dax and saw her walk inside wearing a short pink dress. "And she's fire."

Dax didn't turn to look, his arm remaining around my waist. "You've got a lot of friends."

"Actually, she's my older sister. But she's also a bestie."

Denise came to the table and hugged Matt before she turned to Charlie. "Hey." She hugged him next.

Charlie's arms wrapped around her waist, and he held her, his arms completely covering her body, holding her tight, embracing her much longer than a typical hug.

I waved my hand in front of his face while she looked the other way. "Keep it together," I mouthed.

Charlie gave me a glare before he released her. "Can I get you a drink?"

"Sure. A cosmo would be great."

"Got it." Charlie headed to the bar.

Denise turned to me and hugged me. "You look so good in black." Then she turned to Dax. "Oh geez, you weren't kidding." She looked at me and waggled her eyebrows.

"Dax, this is my sister, Denise."

"Nice to meet you." Dax shook her hand before he looked at me. "Anyone else coming?"

"Nope. That's my crew."

Kat returned from the bathroom and hugged Matt. "Saw a hot guy by the bathroom."

"Ooh, thanks for the lookout." He hugged her back then pulled away. "You look hot, by the way." He gave her a thumbs-up. "Break some hearts tonight. Or break some dick."

She chuckled then fell into a conversation with him.

Charlie came back with the drink and talked to Denise.

I turned back to Dax, my hand sliding over his hard stomach, the chiseled abs underneath that soft cotton. "You shaved."

"You like it?"

"The shadow is hot, but I like it this way too."

His arm curled around my waist again, and he pulled me close. "How's that article coming along?"

I rolled my eyes. "The sleazebags don't want to talk. But that's fine. I've hit up the banks and talked to a few people there. I've got enough for the article, but I'd really like to pack it with quotes and as many incriminating facts as possible."

"You sound more like a detective than a writer."

"You have to be sometimes."

"You're fearless. Pretty sexy."

"Yeah?" My arms moved around his neck, and I held him close.

He nodded. "I can see you've mentioned me to your friends."

"Oh, I've been talking about you all week. I would hope you've been doing the same."

His hand flattened against the curve in my back, taking up most of my body. "I'm not really a kiss-and-tell kinda guy."

"Then what do you talk about with your friends?"

"Sports, current events, the best kind of whiskey..."

"Really? Well, I'm the kiss-and-tell kinda woman, so they're gonna hear all the details."

The corner of his mouth rose in a smile. "You're gonna have a lot of good things to say."

"Good answer." My hand slid up his chest and shoulder and I cupped the back of his neck, my fingers stroking the short strands of hair in the back, and I stepped in closer, letting my lips land lightly on his mouth.

His hand instinctively tugged me near, his soft mouth opening slightly for mine, giving me a sample of a phenomenal kiss. He felt my bottom lip between his and gave me a slow and seductive kiss, a gentle breath, before he kissed me again, this time his hand slipping into my hair, his large fingers cupping my neck. He gave me a final kiss, a touch that made me numb from the lips down, an embrace that silenced the loud music around us, the conversations from other customers. When he pulled away, his eyes stayed on my mouth, like that kiss was as satisfying to him as it was to me.

My hand moved to his wrist, my fingers wrapping around his hardness, my lips slightly open as I lifted my gaze and looked into his. The kiss was short and simple, but it floored me, made my knees go weak, made me anxious to get this dress off and feel him deep inside me. "That was nice."

His eyes flicked up to mine. "Honey, you ain't seen nothing yet..."

WE ENTERED the empty apartment and headed to my bedroom.

I had a queen-sized bed and a dresser with a closet, not much room for anything besides sleeping and getting dressed. But it was big enough for the two of us to enjoy each other, to grab each other hard and kiss with hungry lips.

His hand pulled down my zipper and got the dress loose, letting the fabric fall off my body until it pooled on the floor at my feet.

His hand was in my hair, fisting the strands as he kissed me hard, breathed into my mouth with a quiet moan. He gave me his experienced tongue, moving around mine and taking my breath away.

God, I knew this was going to be good.

My hand grabbed his t-shirt and pulled it over his head, revealing his chiseled torso, the endless grooves between powerful muscles and his lean frame. With parted lips, I stared at his body like I was looking at a model on a fitness magazine. "Oh wow..."

His eyes were on me, seeing the skintight, black lingerie. He inhaled a deep breath, his eyes darkening in a deeper form of lust. It was a black bodysuit made of thin lace, showing my nipples through the fabric, my belly button piercing, the opening between my legs so he could fuck me without taking it off. "Fuck yeah." His voice was deeper and more rugged, so sexy. His eyes roamed over my body until they lifted to mine again.

My mouth moved to his chest, and I kissed his tanned skin, his strong pectoral muscles, dragging my tongue along a cord in his neck. My hands got his jeans loose at the same time, pushing them over his narrow hips and his tight ass. I pushed his boxers down too, getting him buck naked, his cock the monstrous size I'd been hoping for. "Yum..." My hand wrapped around his length and I massaged his hardness, my thumbs gliding over the thick vein, loving the searing heat from all the blood that filled his big dick.

His hand moved into my hair again, and he kissed me while he felt me rub him, my thumb moving over the tip where he'd started to drip. He backed me farther into the bed, anxious with desire.

I ended the kiss, looked into his dangerous eyes, and then lowered myself to my knees.

He released a deep breath, his hand immediately grabbing my hair and keeping it off my face, like he was ready to dive between my lips and glide over my tongue.

I pointed his dick at my mouth then kissed his tip, my eyes locked on to his heated gaze. I kissed his head the way I kissed his mouth, a slow start, an innocent embrace. Then I pushed him into my throat, feeling his thickness occupy my entire mouth, making it difficult to breathe right away.

He closed his eyes and moaned, his features tightening, his breath coming out shaky.

I flattened my tongue and kept going, moving at a slow pace so he could just enjoy it without needing to explode. I liked to be selfless in bed to see how he would respond. It was basically an interview to see if he was qualified to be a regular. If he gave what he received and cared about getting me off, then he made the cut.

I really wanted this man to make the cut.

He started to thrust into my mouth, moaning when he watched me take all of him, his breaths becoming shakier as his face tinted a beautiful red color. His fingers gripped my neck, and he steadied me as he pulled his dick out, like he couldn't take much more of it. His hand gripped mine, and he helped me to my feet before he backed me onto the bed. His hands gripped my hips and lifted me up, bringing my ass to the edge of the bed.

He fished a condom out of his jeans before he rolled it on. But instead of fucking me, he moved to his knees on the rug and buried his face in the opening of the lingerie.

"Oh yes…" My head rolled back, and I closed my eyes, loving his manners.

And he was so good at eating pussy. He was a goddamn professional.

His tongue circled my clit before he sucked on it, applying the right pressure, the right wetness, the right everything.

It brought me close to the edge. "Right there...a little more."

He circled harder, going and going.

My hand dug into his hair as I came, pressing my pussy into his face, moaning so loud Charlie would hear us if he were home. Tears formed in my eyes because it was so good. I whimpered like I was about to sob. "Dax...yes." I rolled my hips and finished, feeling the electrified burn in all the nerves in my body.

He got to his feet, his lips shiny from my wetness. His large hands gripped the backs of my thighs, and he opened me wider, positioning himself at my entrance so he could slowly push his head inside me.

He was so fat...I loved it.

With his eyes locked on mine, he inched farther, making his way through my tightness, parting my channel so he could dominate my wet flesh. He moved deeper and deeper, getting himself completely sheathed with the exception of his balls.

My hands gripped his wrists, my knees parted and were close to my torso, completely open so he could fuck me as savagely as he wanted.

And that was exactly what he did.

He fucked me hard, deep, and mercilessly.

"Yes...yes..." I didn't know how many times I said that word throughout the night. It was always on my lips, always on my tongue. He made me come with his mouth and then again with his dick, driving me into a climax that made me buck my hips and praise the fucking lord. "Oh Jesus..."

When he couldn't last a moment longer, he shoved himself inside and filled the condom, his expression even darker in the throes of pleasure. His cock twitched inside me at release, reminding me just how big that monster cock was. His fingers relaxed on my hips, and he breathed through the high, falling back down to the bed until his cock started to soften inside me.

I pulled him to me, bringing his body on top of mine, and I cupped the back of his neck as I kissed him, tasting myself on his mouth. "You can fuck me like that anytime..."

HE LAY beside me in bed, the sheets at his waist, his chest still slightly shiny from the sweat.

I was still in my lingerie because lingerie was so much sexier than just being naked. My hand moved up his chest, feeling his hardness even when he was fully relaxed. My fingers touched the grooves between his hips, the veins that formed below his navel. I'd invited him to my place so I wouldn't have to walk home after, especially when I was satisfied and exhausted.

I got out of bed and peeled off the lingerie before I pulled on sweatpants and a t-shirt. "I'll walk you out."

He turned his head slightly my way. His expression still showed his fatigue, but he seemed surprised I wanted him to leave. But he got out of the bed and got dressed.

I didn't like sleepovers. I preferred to wake up the next morning and start a new day, not continue from the day before.

We left my bedroom and walked into the living room.

Charlie was standing in front of the fridge, peering inside, like he was looking for a snack after drinking all night.

Dax hesitated for a second when he saw him, turning his head to look at Charlie, but he kept walking, meeting me at the door.

I opened it and stepped into the hallway.

He joined me, looking down at me now that my heels were gone and I was half a foot shorter. His hair was messy from the way I'd fisted it so much, and his eyes fell a little, like he was tired.

"So...can I be a regular?"

He cocked a single eyebrow.

"You know, one of your top girls who can text you for a good time."

He was quiet for a long time, as if he were caught off guard by the question. "That's all you want?"

"Uh, that wasn't obvious?" I asked with a laugh. My hands moved up his chest until they cupped his neck. I moved in and kissed him.

He kissed me back, his kiss as good as before. His arms circled my waist, and he pulled me close, his fingers digging into my ass.

"I'll take that as a yes." I pulled away and dragged my hands down his chest.

His eyes shifted back and forth slightly as he looked at me. "What makes you think I have regular women I hit up for sex?"

"Are you married?"

"No."

"In a relationship?"

"No."

"Then why wouldn't you? Look at you." He was sex on a stick, rocking a perfect dick and an even more perfect smile.

"You have regulars?"

"I'm not married or in a relationship, so yes. But I have a feeling you're going to be my favorite."

He didn't have a reaction to that, didn't show disappointment or amusement. He was impossible to read.

"I just like to be upfront with my intentions. Because I want to see you again...but there's only one reason I want to see you again." I grabbed his shirt and pulled him in for a kiss before I walked back into my apartment. I shut the door without looking at him again.

A man like that wasn't interested in monogamy, and neither was I. The best way to keep him around was to tell him he wouldn't get a clingy woman on his hands, a woman who would want more, want love. Once the foundation was laid down, I could keep him for a long time...and I wanted to keep him as long as I could.

FOUR
CARSON

I walked over to Sugar and Cream, a boutique coffee shop really close to my office, and stepped inside.

Kat waved from her seat, getting my attention in the sea of people with their laptops and paperwork. Other people were meeting friends on their breaks, picking at their muffins and cookies before dunking them into their coffee.

I walked to her table and took a seat. "Aww, you already got me a coffee." I took a sip. "It's perfect. Thank you."

"You got my lunch last time. Aaaannnnnd…I have some exciting news."

"Ooh, what?"

She held up the muffin. "I got the last coffee cake muffin—just for you."

"Bitch, I love you." I took it from her hands and bit right into it, taking a huge bite.

She laughed. "Bitch, I know."

I chewed more than I could handle, getting crumbs everywhere. "It's so good. Fresh."

She grabbed her coffee and took a drink. "How's the office?"

"Just working on my stupid article. Vince keeps lighting a fire under my ass. You can't rush a piece of this magnitude." I kept eating, caring more about the muffin than the steaming cup of coffee with cream and sugar. "How about you?"

She shrugged. "Work is fine. Shopping for super-rich people isn't as interesting as it sounds."

"Really? It sounds super interesting."

"My long-term clients are predictable, so I just drop off their clothes and rarely hear from them. They don't like to reinvent themselves. They just wear the same thing."

"Because they're billionaires. Billionaires don't have time to nitpick at their clothes. They have to run a business."

"True. So, what happened with you and that gorgeous man on Saturday?"

"We fucked. And fucked good."

She laughed, covering her mouth so she wouldn't be too loud for the people around us. "That sounds nice."

"He's such a good kisser. He rarely talks. He's got a big dick... I could go on and on."

"Please do." She held her cup with both hands, leaning forward slightly to hear all the details.

I laughed before I took another bite of the muffin. "I went down on him first, just to set the tone, and he returned the gesture."

"Oh my god, a gentleman."

"Yes. A knight in shining armor. So, that was a really good sign. He worked it until I came."

"Now he's an American hero."

I laughed. "And then he nailed me like a sailor on leave."

"Oh...so romantic." She sighed loudly, as if in longing. "When are you seeing him again?"

"I asked if I could be one of his regulars. He agreed to it."

"You think you'll make the top three?"

"Girl, you know I'm ambitious. I'm trying to make it to the top—no pun intended."

She laughed. "Oh, I love you. You're so free and happy...and I'm happy for you."

My smile waned for a second, the comment hitting me unexpectedly. But then I forced a smile and pretended it hadn't happened.

"What about Boy Toy #1?"

"He's still there, but he just got bumped to economy."

"Poor guy. Does he know?"

"Nah. He's got his own girls, so I doubt he'll care much." I took a piece of the muffin and dunked it into my coffee.

"Dax is so good-looking. He looks like one of those underwear models plastered on the billboards in Times Square."

"I know, right? I can't believe how lucky I am to have found him."

"Looks like you were in the right place at the right time." She drank from her coffee.

"Cupid must have been in that bar with his bow and arrow. So, are you seeing anybody?"

She shook her head then opened her brown recycled bag and pulled out a small sandwich. "I've been so busy with work and stuff…so not really."

I watched her eyes drop, watched her immediately fall under an invisible cloud of misery. "I'm sorry, Kat…"

She gave a weak chuckle, packed with sarcastic pain. "I can't help it. I can't change the way I feel. I can't stop hoping…that we might get back together. Maybe we're one of those couples with a really long love story."

I didn't have the heart to tell her about Charlie's feelings for Denise, that she was the one he couldn't shake off, the one he couldn't forget about. It didn't matter how many women he slept with, how many beers he drank. Denise was the thorn in his side that was so deep he couldn't remove it without bleeding out. With the three of them, I felt like I was in a Shakespeare play, the opposite of a love triangle. Kat was the reason Charlie wouldn't go for Denise, because it would affect the entire group…and someone would leave. Since Denise was my sister, that person was probably Kat, and he just couldn't do that to her. "I think you should get on some dating apps and get back out there."

She rolled her eyes. "Those guys only want one thing…"

"And is that a bad thing?"

"I want a relationship."

"But you're in no state to have one. You need to get over Charlie first. A good first step is spending time with other men, seeing what else is out there. Charlie is a great guy, but he's kind of a doofus. You can do better."

She rolled her eyes. "You don't mean that."

No, I didn't.

"He's your best friend for a reason."

"You're my best friend too."

She chuckled. "You're a best-friend whore. You're best friends with everyone."

"That's not true," I said in mock offense. "Dax and I definitely aren't best friends—based on all the things we do."

WHEN I WALKED in the door, Charlie was making dinner in the kitchen. I had the nose of a bloodhound, so I knew exactly what was on the menu at the first sniff. "Yes, I'm starving." I carried my satchel to the round dining table and set my stuff down.

"Why do you assume I'm cooking for two?"

"Because cooking for one is impossible." I pulled out my laptop and opened it. "And you love me, motherfucker."

He chuckled then carried the plate of food to me. It held three chicken tacos with cilantro, salsa, and a few limes, with rice and beans on the side. "Wow…you really do love me."

He grinned then headed back into the kitchen.

I deepened my voice, sounding like a man who had just come home to his wife after a long day at the office. "Grab me a beer, would you, sweetheart?"

He grabbed two and carried his plate to the table. He set everything down, twisted off the cap, and placed it beside me.

I grinned and pulled it close. "Thank you."

A smile still on his face, he sat down and started to eat.

"I'll do the dishes."

"You bet your ass, you will."

I worked on my computer while I ate, getting right back to work like the walk from the building to the apartment had just been a break. "How's your piece coming along?"

"I'm finished." He grabbed a folder and pushed it toward me. "Rip it apart."

"Will do." We fact-checked each other's work and proofread it to death. It was frustrating to work so hard on something just to see your friend tear it down, but every word we wrote mattered, and making sure it was as good as possible was essential.

"How was your day?"

"Good. Kat and I had lunch."

He kept eating like her name didn't make him feel anything.

I tried not to talk about their relationship because he clearly wasn't in that place anymore. But we were all friends, which made everything complicated. I'd warned both of them at least ten times not to get together—but no, no one ever listened to me.

"How's Boy Toy #2?"

"I don't know. Haven't talked to him." It'd been almost a week since we'd last seen each other, but he'd stuck it to me good enough that the satisfaction was long-lasting. I didn't need another hit yet.

"So, you're just fuck buddies?"

"Hmm...more like a part-time lover."

"Then you're juggling two guys?"

I didn't want to make an assumption, but the tone in his voice felt full of accusation. I turned away from my laptop and looked at him. "I'm not juggling anything. I have two guys that I like to hook up with. What's the big deal?"

He looked away and never answered.

"Wow, did not peg you as a misogynistic asshole."

"I'm not," he snapped.

"You can hook up with all the girls you want, but when I do it—"

"It's not the same, and you know it."

"Ohh..." My temper had flared, and I was a bull out of a cage with a red flag in front of my face. I slowly shut my laptop. "Because I'm a woman and you're a man."

"No, that's not what I meant—"

"Then you better be clear in the next few seconds because you know how I feel about sexist jackasses. I rip them to shreds, and I'll do the same to you, Charlie." He'd never given me that impression, never made a sexist comment. I gave him the benefit of the doubt, hoping this was a misunderstanding.

He paused for a long time to gather his thoughts. "I wasn't going to say anything because people grieve in different ways. But it's been a year, and you aren't improving. In fact, you're getting worse."

"What are you talking about? I'm working, I go out on the town all the time, I'm a *delight* to be around...I'm not grieving. Charlie, I'm just living my life and thoroughly enjoying it."

"That's not what I see. I see someone so shattered that they refuse to feel *anything* at all. You're going through guys like cards in a deck to fill that void, but they're just a distraction from what you actually need to do—which is move on with your life."

"Oh god..." I rolled my eyes.

"I'm serious, Carson." He pushed his food away and leaned closer to me, arms on the table. "You approach everything with sanitizer. You want it to be as meaningless as possible because you're too scared to—"

"Did you ever think that maybe I'm just playing the field... like millions of other people do? I'm young and I'm single. I haven't been single in a long time. It's my time to enjoy it."

"That would be fine, but you haven't been on a single date. You cut right to the chase and don't even give the guy a chance."

"Maybe because I know I don't want to date them," I snapped.

"You don't want to date some hunk?" he asked incredulously. "Some tall, dark, handsome guy you can't stop talking about?"

"I don't know him—"

"That's my fucking point, Carson. You purposely avoid getting to know them. Where does Dax work?"

I shut my mouth tightly, my nostrils flaring.

"His last name?"

"Charlie—"

"Where does he live?"

"This is stupid—"

"You literally know *nothing* about him. And you like it that way."

I pushed my chair back and stormed off.

"Run away, Carson. But you've been running a long time... and you're gonna tire out."

I stormed down the hallway and headed to my bedroom.

"Carson."

I slammed my door and locked it.

FIVE
CARSON

Charlie and I didn't talk for days.

Which was pretty difficult since we lived together and worked together.

Sometimes I had the urge to talk to him about my article or something that happened that day, but then I remembered we weren't talking, and then I grew too stubborn to say anything because he needed to apologize.

But I wasn't sure if he was going to.

I was just about to leave the office when a text message popped up on my phone, from Boy Toy #2.

Want to get a drink?

I hadn't thought about him much, especially after my fight with Charlie. Our falling-out had consumed me every non-work hour of the day. I didn't have time to think about anything else. *Where?*

The place where we met.

I'll meet you in twenty minutes. I could use a drink right now. And sex would definitely help.

I left the office and arrived at the bar ten minutes later. I wasn't in a black dress like last time, but rather a tight pencil skirt and a blouse, with heels. Even though we were just at our cubicles all day, it was still important for us to look professional since our articles were so respected by everyone in the country. But if I had it my way, I'd be in jeans and a top.

I found him sitting alone in a booth, drinking a scotch even though it was barely five. He was in jeans and a t-shirt, his muscular arms propped on the table. His beard had grown in, and now he had a beautiful shadow along his jawline. His eyes were the same color as the booze in his glass.

I smiled as I approached the table. The glass of wine was in front of my spot because he remembered what I'd had last time. "I was taught not to accept an open glass from a man." I grabbed it by the stem and brought it to my lips so I could take a deep drink. "But you can ravish me all you want."

He smiled slightly, but just the subtle rise of his lips was sexy. "I don't need drugs for that."

I smiled before I swirled my glass and took a drink.

"Finished with that article?"

"Not quite. I have a few more interviews this week."

"In back alleyways or by the docks?" he asked playfully.

"I prefer public places, like bars and restaurants. Best way not to get killed."

"You're probably right." He rested his fingers on the top of his glass, shifting it slightly.

"I like a man who drinks."

"Really?" He stared down into his glass for a while, his handsome face so cut and chiseled he had the angles to be a movie star. "I've been told I drink too much."

"As long as you aren't driving or hitting the ER for blood poisoning, what does it matter?" I took another drink, my lipstick smearing against the rim.

"How are you?"

I shrugged. "It's been a tough week. What about you?"

He brought the glass to his mouth, took a drink, and then licked his lips. "It's been alright. Why has yours been tough?"

I didn't want to go into the details, especially when it shone a light on my personal problems. "Charlie and I got into a fight. We haven't talked in a few days."

He stared at me, his elbows on the table and his back straight. He looked so much better naked, but he didn't look half bad in that t-shirt. It hugged his arms just right, molded to his chest perfectly. When he brushed his fingers across his jawline absentmindedly, his sexual magnetism was only heightened. "That must be difficult since you live together."

"Yeah...a bit."

"I was surprised to see him there last week." He didn't elaborate on that statement, just put it on the table.

"I'll never be able to afford to live in Manhattan on my own. Thankfully, our salaries are enough to get us a nice place just a few blocks from the office. But I like living with him, he's a good roommate." I released the breath I was holding, suddenly missing him. "And a great friend."

Dax studied me with those observant eyes, shifting back and forth slightly, catching every hint of emotion on my face. "Close friends are hard to find."

"I know."

"Whatever your problem is, you should try to work it out."

The turmoil was slowly increasing in my chest, making me feel pain for the first time...in a long time. The doors were slightly cracked, and just a bit of emotional baggage peeked through. "You know...I should go talk to him right now." I slid out of the booth and left my glass behind. "I'm sorry to take off on you."

He got to his feet, towering over me, his hands slipping into his front pockets. "I understand."

"Want to come over later tonight? Around eight?" I was usually in bed by ten because I had to get to the office early every morning.

He was quiet as he considered it, looking into my face like the question was surprising to him. He pulled his hand out of his pocket before he rubbed his fingers across his stubble. "Sure."

"Great." I stepped closer to him and gave him a soft kiss on the mouth. "And thank you for the drink."

WHEN I GOT HOME, Charlie had just gotten out of the shower. With a towel around his waist, he saw me in the hallway on the way to his bedroom then pretended like I didn't exist. He shut his bedroom door a little harder than necessary.

I took a deep breath before I followed him. "Charlie—"

"Whoa." He quickly pulled up his sweatpants, covering his junk. "Jesus Christ, knock."

"I've already seen it, so whatever. It's nice, but I'm not interested, alright?" I crossed my arms over my chest.

He grabbed the towel off the floor and rubbed it over his hair, giving it a quick dry before he tossed it back on the floor.

"You've seen me at least twice."

"Not on purpose."

"Well, this wasn't on purpose."

"You saw me walk into my bedroom in nothing but a towel. What did you think was going to happen?"

"I wasn't really thinking about that, alright? You're like a woman to me."

Both of his eyebrows jumped up on his face.

"You know what I mean. There's zero attraction here."

He sat on the edge of the bed, shirtless and in his sweatpants. He had a muscular body, a hardness that Kat had described countless times. He had a handsome face, a fit body, and a good job...so he was a very desirable bachelor. "What do you want, Carson?"

"I-I wanted to talk about our conversation."

He bowed his head and stared at the floor for a while.

"I miss you. I miss my friend."

He closed his eyes for a second. "I miss you too. I'm sorry I attacked you like that."

I'd been hoping for an apology, but it wasn't required for me to forgive him.

"I just worry about you. That's all."

"I know you do, and I appreciate it."

"I'm concerned you're so afraid of getting hurt that you'll never have a meaningful relationship again, and you're gonna keep doing this for years...until it's too late."

"Too late for what?"

"To have kids. To have a husband."

"That's not really a priority for me anymore, Charlie. Who says I need those things anyway?"

"I know you want them, Carson. You're just...emotionally stunted."

I came closer to the bed, staring into his face. "My future is an open book. I don't know what's going to happen. And right now, no, I'm not interested in having a relationship. There's nothing wrong with that."

"I never said there was. It's just...you're going through guys like sticks of gum. You're clearly trying to make yourself—"

"Please don't analyze me."

He shut his mouth.

"I'm not emotionally stunted. I have deep connections with you...my friends. I show and receive love all the time. I trust you with my life. I have everything I need from you guys—except some good D."

He chuckled quietly.

"So, your assessment is wrong. There's nothing wrong with me. I'm fine."

He stared at me.

"I appreciate your concern, but really, I'm fine. I'm only interested in a physical relationship right now, and like lots of other men in their twenties, there's nothing wrong with that. So, don't worry about it."

He nodded. "I'm always here if you need to talk...because you've never talked about it."

And I never would. "There's nothing to say, Charlie. I've moved on with my life. I'm in a good place. I'm one of the top journalists at the fucking *New York Press*, I've got great friends in my life, and I'm banging some ridiculously hot piece of ass. I'm good, alright?"

He smiled. "Alright."

"By the way, he's coming over tonight. Might want to get out your headphones."

He issued a quiet laugh along with a cringe. "Thanks for the heads-up."

SIX
CARSON

Shortly after eight, a knock sounded on the door.

"Ooh, special delivery for me."

Charlie had his feet up on the table as he watched TV, wearing a t-shirt and sweatpants. A beer was on the table beside him, and he was texting on his phone. "Is it a pizza?" he teased.

"What if it's Dax holding a pizza? Man, that would be the hottest thing ever." I walked to the front door and opened it, revealing him standing there in the same clothes he'd been wearing at the bar.

His dark eyes looked into mine like he hadn't just seen me a few hours ago, taking in my appearance with obvious desire, as if he liked the way I did my hair and makeup or he liked the tightness of my shirt.

I grabbed the front of his shirt and pulled him into me, bringing our mouths close together for a hot kiss right in the entryway. My hands moved up his chest and then around his neck, kissing him with long and deep kisses, grateful to be reunited with that incredible mouth.

Man, he was such a good kisser.

Both of his hands slid into my hair, pulling it from my face, handling me delicately and possessively at the same time.

I spoke against his lips. "I can't wait to get on that dick..."

He looked down at my mouth, as if he couldn't believe those words had left my mouth.

I grabbed his hand and interlocked our fingers as I pulled him through the living room and to the hallway.

Dax noticed Charlie on the couch and turned to him. "Hey."

Charlie raised his hand. "Hey, man."

He looked at Charlie for a few more seconds before he turned back to me.

I took him into my bedroom and undressed him, getting every piece of clothing off until he was just a naked hunk. "You're so fucking hot. Oh my god." My hands glided up his chest until I cupped his face and kissed him again.

His big hands moved to my body, and he undid my jeans before he pushed them over my ass. His fingers slipped between my legs, sliding underneath my panties, and he rubbed my clit as he kissed me, his big fingers making my knees shake.

My fingers dug into his hair as I kissed him harder, pausing to pant, moaning when I felt his fingers become coated with my moisture. I pulled my shirt over my head and unclasped my bra as I pulled him to my bed. "Babe, I'm wet for you the second you walk in the door."

He moaned against my lips, like the dirty thing I'd said really got him hot.

I guided him onto my bed, climbing on top of him as he lay back. His head hit my pillow, and his hands gripped my hips.

I grabbed the condom on my nightstand and rolled it down to his base, loving the way his fat dick stretched the latex to capacity. Then I straddled his hips, sank down his length as I bit my bottom lip, and started to ride.

His entire body tightened in pleasure, his muscles flexing instinctively. He clenched his jaw as he suppressed the loud moan that came from his throat. Redness tinted his face, and he looked so sexy just lying there, his fingers digging into my hips as he guided me up and down.

I arched my spine, pushed my shoulders back and stuck out my chest, bouncing my tits up and down as I moved, knowing he would like it.

When he moaned, it was obvious he did.

I was in dick heaven, enjoying his body, using it to give myself the sex I craved. Good sex and orgasms didn't have to be a myth. You just had to hunt for the right man to give them to you. Dax found me in the bar, but I was the one who sank my claws into him and made him mine. I turned him into exactly what I wanted, a sex god who came to my call, a man who knew his place in my life.

"Fuck…" He thrust his hips and fucked me back, driving his dick deep inside me, working up a sweat when he could just lie there and take it. But he wasn't a lazy fuck. He liked to put in the time, energy, and work to make it good.

"Slow down." My hands planted against his chest, and I leaned forward, rocking my hips dramatically, grinding my clit against his hard body, right over the veins that rose up his body from his dick. "Yes..." I flipped my hair to one shoulder and rolled my hips over and over, my eyes locked on his, watching him watch me, watching him breathe hard as I got myself off. It only took a few seconds to make my hips buck uncontrollably, for my moans to fill my bedroom and the hallway, for a wave of heat to cover my body with a new layer of sweat. "God...yes." I ground into him harder, my pussy squeezing him as I came, covering that condom with my cream.

When I finished, I straightened, his hands gripping my ass cheeks and pulling them apart, and I bounced again, going hard, making my tits bob up and down, my lips parted because I was still moaning from the high that hadn't quite faded yet.

"Jesus fucking Christ." He squeezed my hips hard and yanked me up and down, his hips thrusting up to meet me every time I slammed down. All the features of his face tightened as he came, making him so masculine with that shadow on his chin, those dark eyes, that clenched jaw...and that sweat. "Fuck yes." He came with a groan, tugging me down so he could shove his entire dick inside me, releasing into the tip of the condom like he was actually releasing inside me.

I loved watching him come. He looked so sexy every time. I rolled my hips slightly as he caught his breath, feeling his dick slowly start to soften. I leaned over and kissed him, tasting his sweat as well as mine.

Then I got off him and handed him the tissue box. "Good job."

He rolled off the condom, wiped off, and then lay there. "You did all the work, sweetheart."

"Yeah, but you gave me a reason to work." I got back into bed on the other side, keeping space between us because we were both hot and sweaty. I turned over and faced the other way, my ass and back to him.

His hand went to my ass, and he rested it there, his fingers squeezing one cheek. "Your body is beautiful."

I smiled as I kept my eyes closed. "You can thank Pilates for that. What do you do?"

"Running and weights." His hand moved up to my back then followed the curve from my waist to my chest. His fingers moved farther up until they went into the back of my hair, lightly touching the strands. "You two made up?"

"Hmm?" I was already starting to fall asleep.

"You and Charlie."

"Oh...yeah. We talked it out. We're fine now."

"I'm glad." His hand returned to my ass. "I was surprised—"

"I don't mean to be rude, but it's getting late. Can you let yourself out?" I didn't want to do pillow talk. I just wanted sex. It was like a hair appointment. Get in and out in thirty minutes. No reason to overthink it.

He was still for a while before he pulled his hand away and got out of bed. He picked up his clothes from the floor and pulled them on. When he was ready, he walked out of my bedroom and shut the door behind him.

I fell asleep almost instantly.

DAX GRABBED the bowling ball then carried it to the lane.

"That is one tight ass..." Denise nudged me in the side.

Charlie's gaze shifted to hers.

"One gorgeous ass," Kat said.

"Man, I love denim." Matt stared with the same intensity, not caring about his bowling abilities at all.

Dax got a strike, so he was actually pretty good.

But none of us cheered, still mesmerized by that excellent ass.

"Yay!" I clapped and nudged Kat in the side.

"Oh yeah." She clapped with everyone else. "Good job!"

He wore a slight smile, as if he knew exactly what happened like he had eyes in the back of his head. He came back to the spot beside me and took a seat.

Dax's head was turned my way, and he stared at me.

When the stare became impossible to ignore, I turned to face him and met his look.

His arm moved over the back of my shoulders, and he kissed me. It was simple and short, but coming from him, it was so sexy. With those rugged lips, his kiss was practically deadly. "I read your article."

"Which one?" My eyes narrowed in surprise because I hadn't expected him to take an interest in my work.

"All of them. But I'm referring to the one you did about ISIS, how they originated because of the war with Iraq, how they've grown in power, how their presence has completely changed the country and created a problem no one could have foreseen."

Wow, so he'd read the whole thing. "What did you think? And don't worry, you can't hurt my feelings."

"I believe that." He wore a slight grin like he'd made some kind of joke. "You're a great writer."

"Yeah?" I asked, loving positive feedback because I thrived on it. If someone disagreed, it turned into a debate that lasted hours. But when someone praised me, it was music to my ears.

"Yeah. I read the paper every day, so I'd already read your articles over the years. But I went back and refreshed my memory."

"You read the paper?" I asked in surprise.

"A lot of people do."

"I know... I'm just surprised you do."

He stared at me for a long time, the sound of balls colliding with pins in the background, the pop music over the speakers. "Why? You don't know anything about me."

Touché. "Well, thank you for the compliment. It means a lot."

He continued to stare at me, like this wasn't over. "Do you want to know anything about me?"

"Sure. What sport do you follow religiously? Mine is basketball."

He stared at me with his serious eyes, like that question was off-putting. "Football and baseball."

"Ooh…I love baseball. We should go to a game—"

"Do you want to know anything real about me?" The question wasn't hostile, but his eyes burned into mine as he urged me forward, as he pushed my buttons and purposely made me uncomfortable.

"Oh, look." I pointed to the scoreboard. "My turn." I got out of the chair and grabbed my ball. I only hit a few pins, but I'd never been good at the game. I just enjoyed playing it. When I returned to my chair, I assumed that awkward conversation was over.

But he didn't let it go. "You don't care what I do for a living? What if I'm a janitor?"

"Is there something wrong with being a janitor?" I asked, raising an eyebrow.

His features slowly changed, as if he didn't expect me to say that.

"Whether you're a janitor or some suit on Wall Street, it doesn't matter to me. If you want to share your life with me, you're always welcome. But no, I don't care about how you earn a living."

"You're up, Dax," Charlie said.

Dax continued to sit beside me, looking me in the eye and ignoring my friends as they watched us. Then he leaned in and kissed me before he got to his feet and walked to retrieve his ball.

And we swooned over his ass again.

WHEN WE FINISHED with our games, we said goodbye and parted ways.

"I'll see you back at the apartment." Charlie gave me a high five before he headed up the street with Matt.

Dax looked down at me, his arm curling around my waist and pulling me close.

It was hard to look at this man and not think about sex. A man that beautiful was supposed to make all women around him wet, make their ovaries scream, make them desperate to have him.

I grabbed his hand and pulled him away from the street, taking him into a dark alleyway.

"Where are we going?"

I pulled him behind a dumpster, putting my back to the wall and tugging him close. My hands went to his jeans and got them undone.

"Your apartment is just a few blocks away."

"But I want you now." I pulled his jeans and boxers down slightly until his cock popped out. He could pretend he wasn't into this, but his hard dick said otherwise. I lifted up my dress, pulled my thong to the side, and hooked my leg around his hip. My hand cupped the back of his neck, and I pulled him in for a kiss, kissing him hard, kissing him like I'd never wanted a man more. "Fuck me, Dax."

His fingers dug into my bare thigh, and he moaned against my mouth, getting rock hard at the spontaneity and the dirty talk. He ground against me as he devoured my mouth, and a few minutes later, he pulled a condom from his pocket and rolled it on.

I knew a man like him carried protection everywhere he went—because he could get laid at any moment.

He shoved himself inside me and fucked me hard against the wall, the sounds of pedestrians and cars on the main street loud. Sirens went off in the background, an ambulance speeding down the street. The city was never quiet, so our moans and grunts were drowned out.

I held on to his shoulders as I felt him pound me against the wall, my lips pressing into his neck to silence my screams when he made me come. "Dax...yes." My mouth moved to his ear, and I panted. "Yes...yes...god."

He grunted as he fucked me harder, coming a few seconds later. He gripped me hard as he finished, pumping inside me while he filled the condom. He lingered for a few moments before he pulled away, revealing that hot, lustful expression in his eyes, like fucking me in the alleyway only made him want to fuck me again.

Like the lady that I was, I readjusted my panties, pushed down my dress, and then fixed my hair like nothing happened.

He rolled off the condom and tossed it into the dumpster, which was convenient. Then he pulled up his bottoms and adjusted himself like he hadn't just had hot and dirty sex a minute ago.

I grabbed his hand and pulled him out of the alleyway. "Come on, let's get a hot dog. I'm starving."

SEVEN
CHARLIE

THE GIRLS WALKED AWAY AND HEADED TO THE DANCE floor, all three of them immediately standing out because they were beautiful and fun. They spun around and took up more room than they needed because they were the life of the party.

I watched Denise in her black dress, the way it hugged her sexy curves in all the right places. Carson was a thin brunette, with green eyes and fair skin. Denise was blond with blue eyes, and she looked so different from Carson, it was hard to believe they were related. That was probably why I found Denise sexy and Carson...like a little sister who could throw a good punch.

Matt slapped me on the back. "Dude, there're a ton of other women to drool over. Forget about her."

Dax had been staring at them too, his eyes focused on Carson. But now, he turned to me, his hand wrapped around his short glass of scotch. He stood across from us, in an olive-green t-shirt and black jeans.

His expression was difficult to read, but I wanted to make sure he didn't make the wrong assumption. "He's talking about Denise."

Dax took a drink before he licked his lips. His expression was exactly the same, so maybe he hadn't assumed we were talking about Carson. "Why don't you go for it?"

"It's complicated." I held my beer and glanced at them.

"Really complicated," Matt said. "Charlie and Kat were together for two years before he ended it. Going after Denise will cause a lot of problems."

Dax stared at the girls again, his eyes on Carson, who stopped to laugh about something that just happened. "What's the deal with Carson?"

"Meaning...?" I wouldn't sell her secrets or betray her trust, so I decided to act dumb. There'd been guys before Dax who wanted more and never got it. The no-strings relationship was great in the beginning, but then they realized it wasn't enough.

"She hasn't asked me a single question since we met. That deal." He brought his glass to his lips again and took a drink.

I shrugged. "She likes to keep it casual."

He shook his glass. "This isn't casual. This is sterile."

That was the best description I'd heard.

Matt intervened. "You get to nail a cool, sexy chick. So, I'd just leave it alone."

Dax shifted his gaze to him and watched him for a long time. He was different from the other guys Carson usually brought. He didn't say much, but it wasn't because he was shy. He was clearly confident. He was strong. He always drank scotch and fit into the group without needing to make small talk. "You've had this conversation before."

"A bit," Matt said with a shrug.

Dax looked at me again.

The stare was so intense, I felt obligated to speak. "She's not going to change, so I wouldn't bother."

"And you aren't going to tell me why?" Dax asked.

Matt and I looked at each other before we shook our heads. "Sorry, man. We take our secrets to the grave."

Dax turned back to Carson and stared at her while keeping his hand on his drink. He drank from his glass as he watched, his eyes trained and unblinking. She was a target, and he wouldn't miss. "I've been with a lot of women who say they want something casual. But that never lasts. After they see you for a while, they push for something more. Carson is the first woman I've ever been with who actually means what she says."

I hardly knew the guy, but there was something I liked about him. He was calm and collected, good-looking, carried himself well, like he was a sergeant or something. He didn't annoy us with obnoxious conversation or comments. He was the kind of man that could complement Carson because he seemed supportive of her career rather than intimidated. He found her opinions interesting rather than off-putting. And he didn't look fragile, like he could handle her coldness, could put up with her complications instead of fueling them. "Yeah, she's pretty literal."

He downed the rest of his scotch then wiped the corner of his mouth with his thumb. "I'm gonna get another drink." He left the table and headed to the bar.

Matt released a deep breath, like he'd been holding it for a while. "Man…he's so fucking hot."

THE THREE OF us headed back to the apartment, Carson barefoot because she was going to break her ankle wobbling drunkenly in her heels. She crossed the threshold and threw her heels on the floor. "I hate these fucking things…" Her hands went to her hips, and she looked at them on the floor. "Oh my god, I'm so sorry." She bent down and grabbed them both. "I take it back." She cradled them to her chest and kissed both of them. "I didn't mean it."

I looked at Dax and rolled my eyes.

The corner of his mouth rose in a smile.

Carson put her heels on the dining table. "My babies…" She petted them like they were a pair of cats.

"Yes," I said sarcastically. "Put the dirty-ass shoes that you wore all through Manhattan on the dining table."

"These dirty-ass shoes cost me a fortune," she snapped. "They're more expensive than the table."

"If that's true, then you need to change your priorities." I set my wallet and keys on the counter.

Carson turned to Dax and locked her arms around his neck before she kissed him. "Come on, stud. Let's go have sex." She grabbed his hand and started to pull him toward the hallway.

He dropped her hand. "I'm gonna take off."

"What?" She turned back, her eyes open and livid.

"I just wanted to make sure you made it back in one piece."

"I have Charlie for that," she argued. "You're my D dealer."

I rolled my eyes because I couldn't believe the shit that came out of her mouth sometimes.

"You give the best D in this city," she continued. "Come on." She grabbed for his hand again.

He smiled as he circled his arms around her and held her close. "Another time."

"You don't want me?" She pouted her lips.

"I do." He kissed her on the mouth. "I'm just don't want to sleep with a drunk woman."

She rolled her eyes. "Oh, come on. You aren't taking advantage of me."

"Goodnight." He released her and headed to the door. "Bye, Charlie."

"Bye." I waved at him and watched him go.

"Ugh." Carson threw her arms down and headed to the fridge to get some water. "He's gonna screw somebody else... Lucky bitch." She downed an entire bottle of water and stumbled to her room to pass out.

EIGHT
CARSON

I stepped into Vince's office. "You called?"

"How's the article coming along?" He shoved all his papers back into the folder and dropped it onto a stack that was growing bigger and bigger as the day passed.

"It's coming..." I shrugged as I stood in the doorway.

"I want to publish it in next Saturday's edition, so it better be coming by then."

Both of my eyebrows almost jumped off my face. "What?"

"Come on, Carson. I gave you this article because I thought you could churn it out quickly."

I stepped farther into his office and shut the door behind me so everyone else couldn't hear this. "This is one of the biggest stories of the year. We can't mess it up. It takes time. If we want it to be as powerful as it can be, it's gotta be a punch to the stomach. I need more time to make that happen."

He shook his head slightly. "What's the holdup?"

"People don't want to talk, not that I blame them."

"Well, give them a reason to talk, Carson." His phone rang on the desk, and he snatched it. "Vince, *New York Press*."

I took my dismissal and left.

AT THE END of the day, I got a text from Dax.

I'm at the bar if you want to stop by.

I could use a drink after the day I'd had. *Sure. See you soon.* I hadn't seen him since that drunken night over the weekend, when I threw my shoes on the floor then apologized profusely. We'd been spending a considerable amount of time together, getting together with my crew then sneaking off afterward. I hadn't called Brian, aka Boy Toy #1, in a while because Dax was the shiny new toy I couldn't put down.

I walked a few blocks to the bar and stepped inside. It was quiet because the after-work crowds hadn't arrived just yet.

Dax was in the same booth near the window, his glass of scotch in front of him while my full glass of wine called my name. He was in a gray t-shirt and black jeans, dressed casually like usual. He was a jeans and tee kinda guy, which was sexy because he had the body to pull it off every time. He didn't need to wear a stuffy suit to be important.

I slid into the booth across from him. My fingers wrapped around the wineglass, and I brought it to my lips for a deep drink, letting that fruity, dry taste of the red wine wash off the bullshit that happened at the office. I set it down, licked my lips, and looked at him.

He sat back against the leather booth, one hand around his glass, his eyes lifted to look at me while his chin was slightly down.

It was such a sexy look on him that I just stared. In Manhattan, beautiful people were everywhere. No one ever settled down because there was an abundance of beauty. Why commit to one person when there was so much to choose from? But Dax was exceptionally gorgeous. "Thank you for the wine."

He gave a slight nod.

"Is that all you ever drink?"

He took a sip before he brought his body forward, coming closer to the table, his elbows resting on the surface. "No. But it's what I prefer."

"I'd drink more scotch if I could. Unfortunately, it only takes a few glasses of wine to turn me into the hot mess that you saw last weekend. Scotch would put me in the hospital for alcohol poisoning."

"The shoes okay?"

"Still a little sassy, but they'll be alright." I smiled. "Thank you for asking."

"I could tell they meant a lot to you."

"I did a big article on Jimmy Choo, and they were given to me as a gift."

"Nice gift."

"Yes, they're gorgeous." I took another drink.

He swirled his glass slightly, looking into my face like he didn't need to speak to have a conversation with me. He was quiet, contemplative, and that made it easy to be around him. He never bored me with pointless conversation.

"I'm sorry I drank so much. For the record, I still would have jumped your bones and done a damn good job."

Those lips slowly spread into a smile, the light reaching his eyes. "I have no doubt."

"Then you should stick around next time."

"Next time, huh? That happens a lot?"

I shrugged. "I wouldn't say a lot..."

He chuckled. "Whatever you say, sweetheart."

I took another drink, watching the lipstick pile onto the same spot over and over, the red stain becoming bolder until it stopped increasing altogether. Now my lips were plain because the color was gone.

"How's the article coming along? Shaking down any more thugs?"

A sarcastic chuckle burst from my mouth. "I'm not some badass vigilante."

"That's not what I saw the night we met."

"Well, my boss actually just lit a fire under my ass because he wants to publish sooner rather than later."

"And that's a problem?"

I nodded. "I don't have everything I need. I could write it now and throw the accusations on the table, but I really want my words to be a sucker punch, to be one of the top hits on Google that morning."

He drank from his glass as he stared at me. "You want your work to be perfect."

"It's all I'm going to have after I'm gone, so definitely."

He took another drink. "I read that you went to Harvard."

I shrugged. "Guilty."

"Impressive."

I shrugged again, unsure what to say to the compliment. I never would have volunteered that information, and that was why I hated the internet and social media. My name was all over the web, and sometimes my educational background was attached to my projects.

He smiled slightly. "Wow...humility. Didn't think you had it in you."

I cocked an eyebrow. "Excuse me?"

He chuckled. "You're a very blunt person."

"Bluntness isn't the same as arrogance."

He gave a slight nod. "You went to the paper right after graduation?"

I didn't understand why he was asking these questions. They had nothing to do with our arrangement, and besides, it was a boring conversation. "Yeah. I started in the mail room then became an intern."

Both of his eyebrows rose. "A Harvard alumnus starts in the mail room?"

"Everyone at the paper has been to a fancy school. That doesn't mean anything. Attitude and perseverance, that's what matters. The people who are too snobby to accept the position go elsewhere, and it's good riddance." I hated stuck-up snobs who thought they were hot shit because of a piece of paper they paid one hundred thousand dollars to receive.

"And then you went from intern to reporter?"

"I had to work my way up like everyone else. When I finally became a full-time writer, I was doing the sections no one cared about until I proved myself. Then I started getting the good stuff."

He stared at me as he hung on every word, as if he was truly interested. "Do you—"

"I don't understand why you're asking all these questions."

His expression didn't change and his body didn't flinch as I cut him off. Now, he just stared, for a very long time, his dangerous eyes looking deep inside me like he could see my soul. "That's what friends do."

"I've got enough friends. I don't need any more."

He was still again, this time slightly surprised by the words that came out of my mouth. Then the corner of his mouth rose in a smile. He tilted his head back and downed the rest of his scotch before setting the empty glass on the table. "The reason I came to this booth the night we met was because I thought your fire was sexy. I liked the no-nonsense attitude. I liked the confidence. You're strong, successful, and sexy. That's all you. But this..." He nodded to me, referring to something in my body that he didn't specify. "This is fear. Fear is not sexy."

My breathing increased slightly, and a wave of heat suddenly came over me. The embarrassment drenched my skin, and I suddenly felt like I was on display, buck naked and covered in scars.

"You're either heartless...or heartbroken. I hope it's the second one." His arms remained on the table, his fingers around his empty glass. He stared at me with those brown eyes, and instead of being the strong and silent man he used to be, he showed his hand...and he was more observant than he seemed. "I'm not asking for more. I'm just asking to be treated with respect. I would have already walked away if I didn't like you. But I do like you. I want to keep seeing you. But this—" he shook his head "—bullshit needs to stop. If you want to keep seeing me, then we need to be friends." He opened his wallet, left a couple bills on the table, and then rose from the booth. "If you're brave enough for that, call me. If not, then have a good one."

I GRABBED dinner before heading back to the apartment.

When I walked inside, Charlie was at the dining table, sitting in just his sweatpants without a shirt. He was leaned forward with his elbows on the table, his fingers twirling in his hair as he stared at the computer.

I set my food on the table and took a seat. After pulling it out of the bag, I opened it and ate in silence, my satchel on the floor beside me.

Charlie straightened and looked at me over the edge of his laptop. "Hey."

"Hey." I pushed my food around with my fork and took a few bites.

Charlie continued to stare at me. The energy from his gaze danced across my face. "Everything alright, Carson? What did Vince say to you?"

My work problems seemed insignificant now. "Charlie... I think you were right." I kept my eyes on my food, replaying the conversation with Dax in my head. He called me out on my bullshit, and I had no defense, no rebuttal. It was one thing for Charlie or my sister to say something, but Dax and I hardly knew each other, and he read me so easily.

"About?"

I shrugged. "Everything..."

He knocked on the table, getting my attention with the sound. "Hey, look at me."

I closed the top of my box and pushed it away. I wasn't hungry anyway. I finally lifted my chin and looked at him.

"What happened?"

"Dax and I got a drink. He started asking me all these questions about work, and I shut it down."

"Why?"

"I just didn't think it was part of our relationship."

"If you can't talk about anything personal, then what are you supposed to talk about?"

I shrugged. "I was pretty rude to him. He said he wanted to be my friend...and I said I had enough friends."

His eyes filled with disappointment. "Yeah, that was a dick thing to say."

I didn't tell Charlie about his other comment, that Dax knew I was damaged, heartbroken, destroyed…or I just didn't have a heart at all. My outgoing personality and wildness didn't hide the truth deep inside. Dax could see it, and that suddenly made me vulnerable. "He basically told me to change—or he didn't want to see me anymore."

Instead of giving me a lecture about the whole thing, Charlie just stared at me, sympathy in his eyes. "Last weekend, he was asking questions about you."

"Like?"

"What your deal was."

"And what did you say?"

"Nothing. But he is surprised how detached you are."

"I thought a guy like him would love that."

He shrugged. "Not sure. It's hard to figure him out."

"Yeah…" That was one of the things I liked about him.

"You know… I like him. He's a cool guy."

"You hardly know him."

"Yeah, but I like what I do know. I think you should call him."

"I don't know."

"Why not?" he asked.

I shrugged. "I'm pretty embarrassed, I guess."

Charlie's eyes fell, like he felt my pain just as I did. "I can see that. But you're strong, Carson. You'll overcome it. And I think this is a good time to slow down…and maybe work on moving forward instead of finding the next distraction."

I WORKED LONG HOURS, interviewing people, chasing down sources, building the article and rewriting it over and over, dodging Vince as he harassed me for the completion of the project.

But no matter how busy I was, I still thought about Dax.

And everything he said.

I sat in my cubicle, one of the last people at the office. The fluorescent lights had drained my energy by shining down on me all day, time was impossible to distinguish when I was surrounded by four walls.

I pulled out my phone and stared at Dax's message box.

I could just cut my losses and move on, but I did like Dax. And Charlie was right. I wasn't afraid of anything, so I shouldn't be afraid of the mirror Dax held in front of my face. I typed out a message. *Can I buy you a drink?* I stared at it for a while before I sent it off. I wasn't even sure if he would text me back.

Why would he text me back?

I set my phone down.

He texted me seconds later. *Scotch. Neat.*

I WAS RARELY NERVOUS, regardless of the circumstance. Put me on a rocket to the moon, and my pulse wouldn't exceed eighty beats per minute. But I sat alone in the booth, my palms a little sweaty, my heart racing more than it should. I had my glass of Bordeaux in front of me, his scotch sitting there waiting for him.

Then he slid into the booth across from me, in his usual t-shirt and jeans. He grabbed the glass, took a drink, and then regarded me with that intense stare. "Let's try this again." He leaned forward toward me, his fingers resting on the top of his glass, his eyes both hostile and kind at the same time.

I knew I should apologize, but that was hard for me to do. Admitting my wrongdoing wasn't the issue. It was just the fact that I'd done something wrong in the first place. I was a kind person who had been on a tough road for a while, and my response to everything around me was to be cold and distant because I was broken. But that wasn't the solution. "I'm sorry...for the way I spoke to you."

He gave a slight nod. "I accept your apology."

I swirled my glass without taking a drink, just needing to do something with my hands, to divert my eyes elsewhere. "Honestly, I thought someone like you would like being with a woman who only wants sex, no talking, no connecting."

"Someone like me?" He rubbed his fingers across his chin, feeling the coarseness of his stubble. "That's quite an assumption since you don't know anything about me." He shifted his glass then brought it to his lips, staring me down.

"Come on." I raised my hand and gestured to him. "You're gorgeous. Gorgeous men don't look to settle down."

"Gorgeous women want to settle down, but that's not you at all."

"Fine. Am I wrong?"

He considered the answer for a long time before he answered. "No."

I rolled my eyes. "So, my assumption was right."

"And the point I made was right."

"Touché."

"I understand you're just looking for a fling. That's fine with me. But I would like your friendship. If this is a friends-with-benefits relationship, we need to be friends first."

"Why do you want to be my friend?"

He picked up his glass. "Because I like you."

"Really? Because you just told me I was rude."

"You were rude. But everything else about you, I do like."

This was the closest I'd ever let a man come to me. The others respected my boundaries, didn't care about my rudeness. They were just happy to get laid. The others who wanted something more were cut loose right away. But not a single one of them had asked for my friendship. "Alright... we can be friends."

He stared at me for a while, his eyes narrowed on my face like he was examining me on a deeper level.

"But to be clear, I am seeing other people. And this will never grow into something deeper."

He smiled slightly. "This guy really messed you up, didn't he?"

I wanted to snap back with a harsh comment, but I kept it bottled inside. "That's not a topic I ever want to talk about."

He nodded. "Fair enough. But just so you know, someone really fucked me up too."

NINE
CARSON

Charlie was in the kitchen when I walked inside. "Hungry?"

I set my satchel on the dining table. "When have you ever asked that and my answer was no?"

"Well, there was that one time..." He stared into the distance as he tried to recall the instance. "Nope. You're right." He smiled and turned back to his cooking.

I joined him in the kitchen and helped him prepare everything. Charlie usually cooked a few times a week, and we ate the leftovers for a couple days. I served it onto the plates then carried them to the dining table.

Charlie left the pots and pans in the sink to be washed later—by me. That was our policy. He cooked and I cleaned. He joined me at the table. "You seem to be in a better mood."

"I just saw Dax."

"Good. You called him." He leaned over his food and ate.

"Yeah."

"How'd that go?"

"We got a drink at the bar, and I apologized...for being a snappy bitch."

"Wow, you apologized?" he asked in surprise. "What a sight..."

"I apologized to you a couple weeks ago," I retorted.

"No. You just missed me so much that you stopped caring how much I pissed you off."

"Yeah...I guess."

"So, you're going to keep seeing him?"

I shrugged. "I told him we would only be friends with benefits, and I would never change my mind. Then he said it was obvious I'd been hurt."

Charlie finished his bite but didn't take another. He just regarded me for a while.

"But he said he's been hurt too, so...there's that."

He continued to watch me. "I really like this guy, Carson."

"You don't even know him."

"Neither do you. But let's get to know him. Let's give him a chance."

I sighed deeply. "I'm not in that place, Charlie."

"And neither is he. So, it's a good starting point."

I took another deep breath, finding it impossible to ever trust again, to ever really feel anything significant for a man again. I just wanted them for necessities, like lust, affection, good sex. But they served no other purpose.

"Maybe nothing serious will ever happen with Dax. But you could use it as a jumping-off point, to get your feet in the water, to start over..."

I did like Dax. And I really liked the fact that he'd been broken too. Maybe we could be friends. Maybe we could help each other. "We'll see what happens..."

"WHAT HAPPENED WITH YOUR BOSS?" Kat asked, standing beside me while holding her drink.

"He hounded me hard." I rolled my eyes. "He wants me to turn in this article, but it's not done yet—"

"You need to just do it," Charlie said. "Vince doesn't care if it's perfect right now. He cares about being the first news outlet that exposes it. You can always write a follow-up later." He stood beside Matt, his dirty-blond hair combed back.

Kat sipped her drink as she stared at him.

"Not to be a dick, but does anyone read the paper anyway?" Matt asked. "Isn't some other company going to paraphrase your article and put it up on Facebook? So, no one will even know that you were the first to expose all of this?"

That made me take a long drink of my cosmo.

Charlie rolled his eyes. "We have lots of subscribers, and people in the industry respect our work. So, yes, people will know that we were the first."

"Ooh...there's your man." Denise nudged me in the side before she nodded to the entryway.

Dax walked inside in jeans that were low on his hips and a t-shirt that stretched across his big pecs. He always stood straight, always carried himself like a powerful man, and his pissed-off expression made him so sexy.

Every woman in the bar stared at him.

"I always forget how hot he is..." My eyes followed him, knowing he hadn't spotted us yet.

"Me too," Matt said with a deep sigh.

"When are you going to set me up?" Kat asked. "If his friends look anything like him... Yum."

Dax turned his head and noticed me with my crew, and there was a slight look of acknowledgment that entered his eyes, and then he quickly glanced down, looking me over with his hot gaze, like he liked the way my ass looked in my dress. He headed my way, his eyes only on me.

"Oh damn..." I'd forgotten how gorgeous he was. When he called me out on my shit, it made him even sexier. I didn't like being told what to do, but when he put me in my place, it was a turn-on. That was probably why I overcame my humiliation and texted.

His arm circled my waist, his large hand feeling my curves and the top of my ass, and he moved farther in until his face was above mine, his head tilted down slightly so he could look at my lips.

I forgot everyone in the room. I forgot about myself entirely. My lips parted in anticipation of the kiss he was about to give me, and my palms immediately went to his chest to feel his hardness. He was so perfect. He was beautiful on the outside and all man on the inside.

He pressed his lips to mine and kissed me, his eyes open, like he enjoyed the sight of my reaction, the way he lit me on fire, the way my body tightened and became wet for him with just a simple touch.

I leaned into him farther, pulling his bottom lip between mine as I kissed him then did it again...and again. My hand cupped the back of his neck, and I kissed him like we weren't in a room full of people.

He didn't pull away, like he didn't care about the stares. His hand slid into my hair, and he grasped it as he deepened the kiss.

"Uh, Carson?" Charlie said. "We're still here..."

I pulled away and let my hands slide down his chest to his waist.

He squeezed my ass before he turned away. "I'm gonna get a drink. You want anything?"

"I'm covered."

He headed to the bar, all eyes on him once again.

I checked out his ass as he walked away. "That is the finest piece of meat I've ever seen."

"Kobe beef," Kat said.

"Are you still seeing Brian?" Denise asked.

"Occasionally," I answered.

"Why?" Denise asked. "Dax is way hotter."

I didn't like having only one single guy on my line. Put too much focus on them. "He is hotter, but we're never going to be serious, so it doesn't matter."

"Does he have a brother?" Kat asked.

"I don't know." I still didn't know anything about him, except the size of his dick and the feeling of his stubble against my inner thighs.

"What about a gay brother?" Matt asked.

"Don't know that either," I said. "I really don't know anything about him."

"Well, you should change that," Matt said. "Because we all want to know."

AS THE NIGHT WENT ON, we dispersed, finding other people to talk to.

That left Dax and me at the table.

He was on his second scotch, unaffected by the booze—at least it seemed so on the outside.

I didn't drink too many cosmos like last time. I made sure my filter was still on, that I would be sober enough to get laid by the end of the night. "Do you have a brother?"

He turned to me, slightly surprised by the question. "No."

"Sorry, Matt…"

Dax chuckled.

"Well, Kat wants to be set up with a relative or a hot friend."

"Well, I have a sister..."

"Nah, she won't be interested."

"She's not attractive anyway, so it doesn't matter."

I smiled, liking the way he teased his sibling.

"I thought Kat was into Charlie anyway."

My smile faded away. "You picked up on that?"

He shrugged and took a drink. "And Charlie is into your sister, right?"

He was very observant. He clearly had above-average intelligence. "Yes."

"Quite the predicament."

Instead of shielding my life from him to keep this relationship sterile, I decided to peel back the layers, include him like a friend...just as he asked. "Kat and Charlie were together for two years."

He gave a slight nod, his brown eyes filling with understanding. "Got it."

"They've been broken up for six months."

"Is Denise the reason they broke up?" He pivoted his body toward me slightly, one elbow on the table. There were a lot of beautiful women in that bar, but he was a gentleman who gave me his full attention.

I almost didn't answer because it was more detail about my life, but I forced myself to adapt, forced myself to get over this hurdle and open myself up again. "She moved here from LA, and that was how Charlie met her."

He gave a slight nod.

"He ended it, but never told Kat the real reason why."

"Damn...that's rough."

"Yeah." I felt bad for everyone involved because no one was happy. Denise was the only one immune to the pain because she didn't know what went on right under her nose. "I'm torn because Kat is my best friend...Charlie is my other best friend...Denise is my sister. I see everyone's point of view."

He watched my face, a smile moving onto his lips.

"What?"

"This is nice."

"What?" I repeated.

"This." He pointed back and forth between us. "You being yourself."

A slight blush moved into my cheeks because it was embarrassing that it was so obvious, that the difference between my guarded personality and my true personality was so obvious to this man.

He took a drink and set down the glass. "What do you think is going to happen?"

"Between the three of them?"

He nodded.

"I really don't know—it's a mess. Kat hopes they'll get back together, so she's kinda waiting and hoping for that."

"And Charlie?"

"He wants to go for Denise, but he knows it'll hurt Kat...and affect our entire group."

His brown eyes were locked on to mine, and he was an incredible listener. He could sit there and just listen…and that was enough for him. His presence was louder than any words he could say. "Do you think Denise feels anything for him?"

"No idea. I've never asked. I don't want to tip her off, so she notices the way Charlie feels."

"You don't think she notices now?"

"My sister is smart but kinda oblivious."

"That's rough." His arm moved around my waist, and he pulled me close, making every woman in that bar jealous because he was with me and none of them. "Since your friends have run off, you wanna get out of here?"

"Please."

He kissed me as he grabbed my ass before he pulled away.

I smiled, loving the feeling of a man gripping me like that, making me feel like a woman with just a simple touch.

"You like that?"

"Definitely."

He grinned then held me to his side as he walked me out of the bar. "Need to say goodbye?"

"No. They'll figure out where we went."

We made it to the sidewalk and walked side by side, moving past the other people as they headed to a club or dinner. New York was a notorious place for crime, but I never felt unsafe, even when I walked home alone in the dark. There was far more charm to this city than people gave it credit for. New Yorkers were standoffish, but they rushed to your aid the second you needed it. For a place filled with nearly two million people, there was a strong sense of community.

"So, where's your place?"

He turned and looked down at me, that sexy grin coming into his features. "Two questions in one night."

I rolled my eyes. "Come on, let it go."

"You do the same thing with your other guys? Never ask them anything?"

"Pretty much."

"And they're fine with it?" he asked in surprise.

"Most. When they start to want more, I kick them to the curb."

"So how do you know those guys aren't serial killers or doll collectors if you don't get to know them?"

I shrugged. "I don't. That's what makes it exciting."

He chuckled. "So, the possibility of me having a doll collection is exciting."

"Oh, you definitely don't have one. I think I've got you figured out anyway. You don't always need to question someone to figure out what kind of person they are."

"Alright. What kind of person am I?"

"Hmm..." My arm moved around his waist as I walked with him. "You're the strong and silent type...so maybe former military?"

He shook his head. "Never enlisted."

"Alright. Then you're probably some kind of business owner."

"Why would you think that?"

"You don't have the coworker vibe. You seem like someone who prefers to be alone."

His eyes were on me, like he was replaying my words in his head.

"Am I right?"

"No." He faced forward and kept walking, navigating the path so I could stare at his profile.

"Then what do you do for a living?"

"Finance." Now his responses were getting short, like he didn't want to talk about his livelihood.

"Yeah, I can see that." I didn't press the topic since I didn't really care what he did for a living anyway. "But you seem like someone who would have a brother."

"Just a sister."

"Are you close?"

"Kinda."

"How can you kinda be close?" I asked with a laugh.

"We talk often."

"Does she live in the city?"

"Yes."

"Does the rest of your family?"

"Yes. Born and raised."

To be able to afford to live in Manhattan that long meant his family probably had some kind of wealth. But he didn't seem super rich. I was around rich bachelors all the time, and they wore watches worth one hundred thousand dollars. Their suits were worth more than a car. All he ever wore was jeans and a t-shirt, so he seemed like a laid-back kind of guy.

"You?"

"I'm originally from LA, but I moved here after college."

"So, your parents are back in California?"

"No. They've passed on."

"Oh…" His gait slowed down a bit, like those words actually wounded him. "I'm sorry about that."

"Yeah…thanks."

"My parents are gone too."

I turned back to him, surprised that he'd been through the exact same thing. "I'm sorry too."

He faced forward again and continued to walk. "Looks like we have a lot in common."

"Yeah, I guess so."

EVERY POSITION with this man was good, even plain missionary. His arms were locked behind my knees, and he drilled into me, making my headboard tap against the wall hard and fast, like the sound of a woodpecker pecking into a tree.

I came all over his dick…over and over.

I loved his powerful body on top of mine, when his sweat rubbed against my tits, when his face tinted red because of the blood, adrenaline, and arousal. He knew how to fuck, how to kiss, how to do it all.

When we were finished, he lay on the bed beside me, naked on top of the sheets, his dick still nice even when it was smaller.

I didn't cuddle, so I stayed on my side of the bed, turned his way with my arm under the pillow.

He looked out the window as he lay there, his breathing slowly returning to normal. The sweat evaporated from his skin as his body temperature went down.

I was getting sleepy, but I stayed awake so I could let him out once he recovered. The sex and the booze created a cocktail so potent that it made me sleep hard for well over nine hours.

"How long have you and Charlie been living together?"

"About a year now." I yawned and closed my eyes.

"How did you meet?"

"At work."

He turned to me. "He works at the paper too?"

"You didn't know that?"

He shook his head. "You worked really hard to make sure I didn't know anything, sweetheart." He smiled slightly, like he was teasing me.

"Yeah. We work together and we live together, so that's how you know we really like each other, to handle each other like that."

"True."

"We both started as interns and moved up. His previous roommate ditched him, so he asked if I wanted to move in last year. The rest is history. We work on each other's stuff, help each other, so we're each a great resource to the other."

"I've never known a writer, and now I know two."

"Yeah." I yawned again. "You know, I'm getting pretty tired..."

"At least you're being nice about it this time." He chuckled then got out of bed.

"I just don't do sleepovers."

"Neither do I." He pulled on his clothes and got dressed.

I rolled out of bed and pulled on sweats and a t-shirt.

"You're going to walk me out?" he asked in surprise. "Wow...the five-star treatment."

I rolled my eyes. "Shut up."

He walked down the hallway, and I followed him. When we got to the door, Charlie walked inside, his eyes heavy from the booze.

"Taking off, man?" Charlie shook Dax's hand. "See you next time." He grabbed a water from the fridge before he went straight to bed.

Dax turned to me to say goodbye. "I'll see you around." He cupped my face and leaned down to kiss me, having to make up for the differences in our height since my heels were off.

"Alright." My hands felt his hard body one more time before I released him. "By the way, Charlie likes you."

"Yeah?" He opened the door and gave me a slight smile.

"Yeah."

"He's a pretty cool guy too." He gave my ass a final squeeze before he left.

SOME PEOPLE THOUGHT the Italian mob was a myth. They had disappeared by the late sixties, early seventies. Organized crime was just crime, regardless of the source or affiliation.

Well, it wasn't a myth.

That shit was real.

I walked into the restaurant, which was empty with the exception of the four men sitting at the table, drinking cappuccinos and speaking in Italian. Cigars were lit, their bellies were fat, and they took up the entire restaurant like they owned the place.

They probably did.

Joe stopped talking and shifted his gaze to me, looking at me from under his bushy eyebrows. "Look who it is, boys." He gave me a pleasant smile even though we weren't friends. We weren't enemies either.

That was why I was still alive. "How was your lunch?"

"Lunch?" Joe asked. "We can't eat lunch at our age, not if we don't want our wives to kill us." He laughed loudly.

The others did too—even though it wasn't funny.

"You look lovely, sweetheart." Without turning around, he gave a command to one of his minions behind him. "Get the lady a chair and a coffee."

A waiter placed the chair beside him. "Here you go."

I took a seat and crossed my legs, in a black dress with my hair curled. "How are you, gentlemen?"

"You know, it's business as usual." He held up a cigar. "Would you like one?"

"Sure. Why not?" I placed it in my mouth and turned to him.

He lit it with his lighter.

I sucked in the air to get it lit, and then the smoke wafted to the ceiling.

The waiter brought my coffee.

"You're too beautiful to be one of the boys, but you're one of the boys." He smiled at me, loving the way I accepted his cigars, the way I joined them and held my own. "So, what can we do for you?"

"Would love some information." I took a puff then let the smoke escape my slightly parted lips. The mob was a mythical legend that still operated, but the police had bigger problems on their hands. Crime had risen over the decades, and now there were bigger fish to catch. These guys were the best sources of information, so it was best to leave them alone. I never wrote articles about them or cited them as a source. "My editor is riding my ass about getting this article live, but I'm missing some pieces of the story. There's a ring of corporate fraud that includes the big players, the Maloney Brothers, Derek Huntington, the Oasis Group... the list goes on."

Joe glanced at one of his guys, had a silent conversation, and then returned to me. "Huntington, huh?"

"Perfect opportunity to throw an opponent under the bus." I took a sip of the coffee and returned to my cigar.

He shook his head. "I know a bit about Derek...and I'm not a fan."

"What did he do to you?"

He shook his head and never answered. "You're going to want to write this down, sweetheart."

I grinned and pulled out my phone, ready to text the story into my notes. "Ready whenever you are, Joe."

TEN
CHARLIE

After work, I went to a bar to meet a source. We sat in a booth together and talked back and forth, but the meeting wasn't as productive as I wanted it to be. Most of the time, I was going from person to person, chasing down the next lead, and after weeks of harassment, I finally found the source that could give me what I wanted.

This guy wasn't the one I wanted.

After I left the cash on the table, I headed out.

Dax rose from a booth, shook hands with some guy in a suit, and then the guy walked out. Dax was in jeans and a t-shirt like always, so he didn't look dressed to do business, but that seemed to be what he was doing.

He was right in my path, so I walked up. "Hey, man."

Dax clearly hadn't expected me to be there because a slight look of surprise came over his face. But then he replaced it with a friendly smile and extended his hand. "Charlie. How are you?"

"Just trying to shake down a source." I shook his hand.

"You sound like Carson."

"That bitch tries to shake everyone down."

He chuckled. "Yeah, she does. Even me."

"So, what are you doing?"

"Just business." He slid his hands into his pockets and didn't elaborate.

I didn't know what he did for a living, and I didn't think Carson knew either. He was shrouded in a bit of mystery, but I wouldn't interrogate him. It was none of my business anyway. "Thanks for putting up with her. I know she's a lot sometimes."

He regarded me for a while, looking into my face with a confident gaze, having a distinguished presence I'd encountered before. Some of my sources were powerful men, and they could say more when they said less. That was what Dax reminded me of. "I think I set her straight."

"She responds to bluntness."

"Because she's blunt." He smiled slightly, like he was playfully teasing her.

I never got involved with the men Carson brought around, but I actually liked Dax. He was easy to get along with, didn't flood conversations with unnecessary words. "I was going to head home and watch the game. You want to come along? Matt is coming over."

He had no reaction to my request for a few seconds. "Let's do it."

"Cool."

MATT WOULD ONLY WATCH the TV for so long before his eyes shifted back to Dax, checking him out without being even remotely discreet about it.

Dax sat on the edge of the couch with his beer on the end table, his ankle resting on the opposite knee. He got comfortable, made himself at home, and talked about the stats like he knew exactly what he was talking about. He seemed more intelligent than the average person, based on all the subtle things he picked up about our group, the way he handled Carson. He just didn't seem average.

I kicked Matt discreetly then glared at him.

He hugged his shin. "Ouch. What the fuck did you do that for?"

"Because you have a staring problem," I whispered.

"Leave me alone. I'm not groping the guy."

Dax smiled slightly, like he wasn't the least bit intimidated by Matt's infatuation. "Seeing anybody, Matt?"

"No...are you bi?"

Dax chuckled. "No. Just curious."

Matt shrugged. "Here and there, but nothing serious."

"I don't have a gay brother, but one of my buddies is. You want me to set something up?"

"Is he hot?" Matt blurted.

Dax shrugged. "He's a good-looking guy, I suppose."

"Maybe we could do a double date," Matt said.

"I don't think Carson would be down for that," he said with a chuckle. "But we can go out for a drink or something. I'll make the introduction."

"Do you have any hot girlfriends?" I asked hopefully.

"I know a lot of hot girls." Dax kept his eyes on the TV. "But none of them are friends..."

So that would mean they would be his leftovers, and that could be awkward.

"I thought you had your eyes on Denise anyway?" Dax turned to me, grabbing his beer and taking a drink.

"Carson told you?" I asked in surprise.

"I picked up on the love triangle a while ago."

I did remember his comments.

"Then I asked Carson for the details," Dax said. "That sucks, man."

"Yeah." It was shitty. If I went after Denise, it would cause problems. If I got back together with Kat, I'd be unhappy. If I did nothing...I would be miserable. "Wait, you got a friend to set up with Kat? I mean, if she's into someone else then forgets about me, it could happen."

"I can ask." He turned back to the TV.

"Perfect," Matt said. "I'm glad Carson brought you around so we can all get laid."

Dax grinned then watched the TV.

The front door opened, and Carson walked inside. She was in a black dress and heels, her hair down in curls. She hung her small purse on the hook by the door and walked farther into the apartment, not noticing Dax as she headed to the computer. "I've got to get a drink to get this bad taste out of my mouth." She grabbed a beer from the fridge, twisted off the cap, and then took a drink.

"Why do you have a bad taste in your mouth?" Matt asked.

She headed into the living room. "Smoked a cigar." She stared at the TV for a while, checking the score and seeing the activity on the field.

"You were with the mob?" I asked, knowing she didn't smoke regularly.

"Yeah." She kept her eyes on the TV as she drank her beer. "Joe gave me some good information."

Both of Dax's eyebrows rose, and he set down his beer. "You know the mob? As in, the notorious Italian mob?"

Her eyes shifted to him on the couch, visibly shocked he was there. "Dax, what are you doing here?"

"I invited him over to watch the game," I explained. "We ran into each other at a bar."

"Oh." She moved to his side of the couch. "I don't know how I didn't see you. I mean, you're the sexiest guy in the room."

"Whoa, excuse me?" Matt pointed at his chest.

"I'm hot too," I argued.

She leaned down and let her knees sink into the couch as her arms hooked around his neck, her dress riding up a bit. She leaned in and kissed him, a short kiss that was still packed with heat. She pushed her palm against his chest and got to her feet before she adjusted her dress. Then she took a seat in the armchair, resting her beer on her thigh.

Dax's gaze was glued to her, indifferent to the game. He grabbed his beer and took a drink, his eyes still on her, like nothing else mattered once she was in his line of sight. He looked at her legs, watched her drink her beer.

I was surprised Carson didn't take the seat beside him, but that was just how she was. Affection was only lustful, and she didn't like to share any other kind. Her heart had been permanently switched to the off position. I was hopeful Dax would get her back into the game, bringing her back from the dead, whether they ended up together or not. He could be her baby steps.

He didn't seem to mind being an experiment.

When the ump called an out, Carson got to her feet and raised her arms like a bear. "What the fuck?" She moved to the TV and screamed at the guy on the field who couldn't hear a word she said. "You're a motherfucking piece of ass, you know that?" She fell back into the chair, shaking her head.

"I hope that's not how you talk to the mob." Dax continued to watch her.

"No." Carson drank her beer. "They're sweethearts."

"The mob are sweethearts?" Dax asked incredulously.

She turned in her chair to look at him. "Well, not all of them, but the ones I know are..."

He still looked surprised, but there was a smile on his lips, like he couldn't resist how comical the situation was. "Why were you hanging out with those guys?"

"They gave me what I needed to finish the article. So, I'm going to finish it tonight and submit that shit first thing in the morning." She turned back in the armchair and looked at the TV again.

Now that she was in the apartment, she was the only thing he cared about. She was the only thing he stared at. His fingers were wrapped around his empty beer, and he didn't get up to grab another, because the view was just too nice.

AT THE END of the game, Carson returned to the kitchen. "What's for dinner?"

"Why do you always ask me that?" I gathered the empty beer bottles and carried them to the recycling can. "I'm not the wife in this relationship."

"Well, I can cook...but you know how that will turn out." She opened the pantry and pulled out a box of mac and cheese.

I rolled my eyes.

Dax dropped his bottles in the recycling can. "Why don't we go out?"

"Depends." Carson was still in her dress, the black material squeezing her hourglass frame, her tiny waist, big tits, and her peach-like ass. Her curves weren't the product of long sessions at the gym, but rather, running around and threatening people for information. "Where are we going to go? Because I'm kind of craving Chinese."

"You always want Chinese," Matt said as he rolled his eyes.

"What do you think?" Carson turned to Dax, one hand on her hip while her arm gripped the edge of the counter. She slipped off her heels, so now she was short in comparison to his tall height. She tilted her head, her hair shifting across her chest.

He looked down at her and said nothing, his eyes roaming over her face, staring at her lips, her cheeks, and then everything beneath that. He was never uncomfortable with his stare, was indifferent to the way he made her feel about it. Seconds passed before he answered. "Chinese is fine."

"I win." She turned to us, victorious.

"His vote doesn't count," I argued. "He only agreed because he's sleeping with you."

"Uh, no." She held up her hand. "That man knows he's gonna get laid no matter what he says."

Dax grinned slightly and dropped his gaze.

"How about Italian?" I asked.

"Yuck." She shook her head dramatically. "I was just in an Italian restaurant, and I associate it with cigar smoke."

"Burgers?" Matt asked. "There's a Mega Shake nearby."

"How about this?" Dax looked at Carson. "We get Chinese. They get whatever they want."

That meant they would eat alone together, which was something Carson avoided at all costs. She hadn't let a man take her out for a meal in a year. She would only spend time with them in very specific settings. But her unease quickly vanished because she knew it was an absurd way to live, that she needed to move on. "Let's do it."

ELEVEN
CARSON

With his elbows on the table and his body slightly shifted forward, Dax stared at me.

I held the menu in front of me, glancing up at his hard expression every few seconds. He was in a classic tee, showing off his tanned skin, the cords over his muscles, his innate sex appeal. "What are you getting?"

"Whatever you're getting."

I dropped the menu. "Well, I like spicy food. Like, *really* spicy food."

"Same here."

"You don't understand, honey." I held up my hand. "I can eat twenty peppers in a row and want more."

A slight smile moved onto his lips, as if he were amused by my attitude. "I'm up for the challenge."

"Alright. It's your funeral." I put the menus at the edge of the table.

"It just means I won't be having pussy for dessert."

My eyes widened at his statement.

He grinned as if he liked that reaction.

With all that hotness on his lips, he wouldn't be able to go down on me, and he was soooo good at it. "Hold on." I grabbed the menu again and searched for an alternative.

He chuckled. "Get what you want, sweetheart. I'll get something else."

"Oh, thank god." I threw the menu back.

The waitress came over and we ordered. He got orange chicken, and I got the Sichuan hot chicken plate. The waters were placed in front of us, and now we were alone again. Only a couple people were in the restaurant, so it was pretty much just the two of us.

He looked out the window for a while before he turned his dark eyes on me. "Does it bother you if I hang out with Charlie and Matt?"

"No," I said immediately. "I don't own them."

"Good. I'm in a basketball league and need a few more players."

"Uh, excuse me?" I crossed my arms over my chest and copped a full attitude.

He stared at me blankly, unsure what he'd done to provoke me.

"I play basketball."

"Yeah?" A slow grin stretched across his face, the kind of smile that reached his dangerous eyes and made him less intimidating. "We're pretty competitive. You think you can handle it?"

"You have no idea."

His smile stayed, like he was truly amused by me. "Fair enough. You can handle the Italian mob, so you can handle this."

"Damn right."

The waitress brought our food and placed it in front of us.

"Oh, this looks good." I grabbed my fork and started to eat.

It was the first time he had eaten in front of me like this, and he pulled his elbows off the table and ate, his masculine jaw shifting as he chewed. He had a shadow on his face, dark and coarse hair that matched his dark eyes. "You've got to tell me, how did you meet the mob?"

"Oh, I hunted them down."

He cocked an eyebrow.

"They're like the godfathers of the city. They just know shit."

"And why are they inclined to share anything with you?"

"Because I never share them as a source. And they think I'm cute."

He smiled before he chewed again. "You are cute."

"And I smoke and drink with them too. They like that."

"Are you a regular smoker?"

"God, no." I shook my head in disgust. "Just a social smoker. It seems like the more I drink and the more I smoke, the more I'm taken seriously. Which is stupid, but whatever. You?"

"You know I drink."

"Smoke?"

"Occasionally."

"To make you look more manly, or because you actually enjoy it?"

He considered the question as he took another bite and chewed it. Once it was down his throat, he answered. "I enjoy it. A flavored Cuban is perfect on the right occasion."

"Like in a strip club?" I teased.

He shrugged. "Sometimes."

I kept eating, feeling the fire on my tongue, and swallowed it down with copious amounts of water.

"Looks like it's too spicy for you."

"Oh no. Definitely not." I kept eating, feeling my eyes water, my sinuses open up and drain like a flood.

He seemed amused but didn't tease me more about it. "Do you feel relieved that the article is finished?"

"No. Charlie has to read it first, which he'll do tonight, and then Vince has to rip it apart."

"Vince?"

"My boss slash editor."

"Well, when it hits the stands, I'll buy a copy."

"Yeah?"

"Yeah." He nodded.

"That's sweet." A guy had never taken much interest in my work before. Dax was the first guy who seemed genuinely impressed by my job, impressed by what I accomplished. My success and ambition weren't a turn-off.

"I just want to brag to my friends about the woman I'm seeing."

"The woman you're *screwing*," I corrected. "We aren't seeing each other."

He took a few more bites and didn't react to what I'd said. "We've made a lot of progress, so I'll let that go."

"What? That's what we agreed on."

"I'm not going to describe you that way to my friends."

"You haven't told them about the way I jump your bones?" I asked in surprise.

He shook his head. "Not the kiss-and-tell type."

"Because you're a gentleman?"

"No. I just don't feel the need to discuss my conquests. Bragging in all scenarios is ugly."

I looked down at my food as I felt the rush in my chest. The more I got to know him, the more I liked him. He was so confident that he didn't need to brag, didn't need to talk about himself to show that he was a man. He had an old soul but a handsome smile. "I like that."

"You talk about me to your friends?"

"Oh yeah. I brag all the time."

He kept eating, his eyes showing his amusement.

"And trust me, they're sooooo jealous." I took a few more bites, became overwhelmed by the spiciness, and had to drink all of my water and some of his.

He chuckled. "You don't have to prove anything to me, sweetheart."

"I'm not. I love it—despite the pain."

"No wonder you get along with my dick so well."

I looked into his eyes as I felt the smile move into my eyes, liking the dirty thing he'd said and the way he pulled it off. "So, when are these games?"

"Every Wednesday night."

"I think I can make that work. But I might have to chase someone down with a club once in a while."

"We've got eight or so players, so that's fine."

"Great. So, you're still going to ask Charlie and Matt?"

"Yeah. Unless you don't want me to."

"I don't mind at all."

"Does your sister play too?"

"No." I kept eating. "She's more of a yoga in the park kind of chick."

"And you aren't?" he asked, staring at me. "Your body indicates otherwise."

I rolled my eyes as if that line meant nothing to me, but I was incredibly flattered. "I don't usually have time to exercise. And I'm just not a fan of the treadmill and weights. I need to chase after a ball to stay motivated."

"Like a dog?" he teased.

"Exactly."

"Did you play ball in high school?"

"And college."

"Really?" he asked, his eyebrows rising in approval. "At Harvard?"

"All four years, honey." I flexed my arms like a superhero. "They called me the three-pointer bitch."

"Now I'm really excited to play with you."

"And your friends better not go easy on me. I can handle an elbow to the face or the stomach. Just not the tits." I rubbed my chest. "I love my girls."

"I love them too."

"Oh, I know…" I smiled before I took another bite.

My phone lit up on the table with a text message, the name reading Boy Toy #1. *What are you doing tonight?*

I grabbed it and texted back. *I'm out with a guy right now.* I set the phone back down and kept eating.

He texted back. *Alright. Talk to you later.*

I liked Brian because he never pushed for more. He was fine with the casualness. When I talked about other guys, he never cared. Sometimes he mentioned the girls he was seeing. The sex wasn't as good and the attraction was nowhere close to what I had with Dax, but he was convenient and didn't cause problems.

Dax kept eating. "Does Boy Toy have an actual name?"

I was surprised he'd read my texts, but it might have been instinctive. We were so used to our phones that whenever a screen lit up, our eyes automatically darted to the words that appeared on the surface. "Brian."

He didn't have a reaction, didn't seem angry or jealous. "You see him a lot?"

"Not as much as I used to. After we met, he kinda became an alternate."

He gave a slight smile.

"What about you? You must have women booking you out weeks in advance."

He'd just finished chewing his bite when he gave a chuckle. But then he kept eating and didn't answer.

"What is your personal life like?" I didn't ask out of jealousy or possessiveness. We were friends because he wanted to be friends, and that was what friends talked about. And now that I'd given him a chance to be a bigger component of my life, I actually liked it.

He finished his plate, only leaving a few pieces. He wiped his mouth with a napkin even though he hadn't smeared anything on his face and pushed his plate away. "There were a few women I was seeing when we met, but not so much anymore."

"Because I'm your new favorite flavor?" I teased.

His eyes narrowed on my face, staring at my features, holding the look for a long time. "Something like that."

I dropped my gaze and picked at my food, full but still eager to keep eating. "I imagine they're all models or trainers or something."

The tab arrived, and he immediately grabbed it and pulled out his wallet.

"We'll split it."

He stuffed the cash inside and returned it to the edge of the table. "I got it."

"Oh, come on. Don't be one of those guys."

"One of what guys?"

"Who insists on paying for everything. We're just friends." I grabbed my cash and put it inside, throwing half of his bills back at him.

He didn't fight me and slipped the cash back into his wallet.

"So, models? Actresses?"

"I don't kiss and tell."

"I'm not asking for names."

"Why are you so interested in the type of women I sleep with?"

"Because you're the hottest guy in the world," I said with a laugh. "I can only imagine the kind of women you've been with. It's kinda a compliment...that I'm in their ranks. It's like when people brag about screwing a celebrity."

He cocked his head slightly, his eyes narrowed. "You're being serious right now?"

"Uh, yeah. Why?"

The waitress took the bill and walked away.

Dax didn't pull his gaze away from my face. His head eventually straightened, and his eyebrows fell. His elbows returned to the table and his hands came together, his shoulders broad and muscular, a vein emerging from the neckline and running to his jaw. He looked down for a second before he gave a slight shake of his head. "Nothing."

I UNLOCKED THE DOOR, and we stepped inside.

Charlie was asleep on the couch, shirtless in his sweatpants with his beer on the end table beside him. The TV was still on, showing a commercial.

I turned off the TV and grabbed a blanket to drape over him to keep him warm. I gave him a gentle pat on the head before I turned off the lamp and took Dax by the hand. We walked down the hallway and into my bedroom.

Once we were inside, I immediately slid off my shoes and got out of my dress, eager to get the skintight clothes off my full stomach. I hung up the dress in my closet and placed my shoes inside.

Big arms circled my waist, a powerful chest pressed between my shoulder blades, and he rested his forehead against the back of my head.

My hands glided down his arms, and I leaned my head back against his chest so I could look up at him.

He was naked against me, his big dick hard at my back. His large hands slid over my stomach and grabbed my hips, his dark eyes looking into my face with that sexy expression.

I turned around and moved into him, getting lost in the quiet moment between us. He was so easy on the eyes, so hard to the touch. A hotter man had never been in this bedroom, been between my legs. My hands planted against his chest and slowly moved down, over the grooves of his stomach. My eyes followed my fingers, followed the ridges and valleys between the mountains of strength.

His hands came around my back then unclasped my bra with a simple movement of his fingers, like there was no bra he couldn't conquer because he'd seen them all. The straps slipped off my shoulders until the entire garment dropped to the floor.

He stared at my chest before he placed his big hands over each breast, squeezing them both, massaging them harshly, like he wanted to hurt me just a bit.

I pushed my thong over my hips and let it fall to the floor.

"I love your tits." His thumbs swiped over both nipples before he squeezed them firmly again.

"I have nice tits."

The corner of his mouth rose in a smile. "Damn right you do." His arms circled my waist, and he pulled me close, his mouth moving to mine.

I pressed my hand against his chest. "Whoa, slow down."

He pulled away but continued to stare at my lips.

"My mouth is pretty fiery..."

His eyes flicked up to meet mine, and then that subtle smile was back, like he enjoyed the fact that I told him what I wanted. That my requests were unapologetic, that I showed no shame.

I'd spent my time being what my man wanted me to be, being selfless, giving more than a hundred percent. But that only got me a broken heart, so I would never do it again. Now I just said what I wanted and didn't wait for him to do it on his own.

He leaned in and kissed me on the neck before he lowered himself to his knees.

I watched him, my breath coming out shaky as he kneeled right in front of me. He was still big and powerful beneath me, his shoulders broad, the veins visible in his thighs. He balanced my hip with a hand and pushed my leg over his shoulders, his lips moving to my pussy with a deep kiss.

My head rolled back, and I dug my fingers into his hair, taking a deep breath as he sucked everything out of me, brought me to the edge instantly like he'd been kissing me for hours. "Dax..."

HE LAY beside me in bed, on his back, still a little sweaty.

I was ready to knock out. "I'm getting tired..."

"Then go to sleep." His hand moved underneath his head, and he closed his eyes.

I gave him a gentle shake. "Come on."

"If you can fall asleep so easily beside me, then I'm obviously not bothering you."

"Dax." I propped myself up on my elbow and looked down at him.

"No."

I narrowed my eyes on his face.

He turned to me, equally authoritative. "I'm tired of heading home at—" he glanced at the time on the nightstand "—midnight. I'll leave first thing in the morning."

"Well, I need to work on my article."

"Right now?" he asked in surprise.

"Unfortunately..." I was going to sleep for an hour then grab my laptop.

He sighed then got out of bed. "Next time, I'm not leaving."

"I thought you didn't do sleepovers."

"It's not a sleepover. It's passing out after good sex." He grabbed his clothes and dressed. His jeans covered his muscular thighs, and his shirt covered his beautiful chest. He smoothed out his clothes then grabbed his phone.

I pulled on a t-shirt and sweats and walked him to the front door.

Charlie was still on the couch, snoring.

I grinned as I walked by and opened the front door. We stepped into the hallway, cracking the door just a bit.

"Does he normally pass out on the couch like that?" Dax asked in a quiet voice.

"Only when he has too much beer."

"So, pretty often," he teased. With his hands in his pockets, he looked at me, his smile fading. "Goodnight." He turned to walk away, not giving me affection before he departed.

I grabbed him by the arm and turned him back to me.

When he turned, there was a slight smile on his face, like he knew he had me right where he wanted me.

I pulled him close and rose onto my tiptoes.

His large arms circled my waist, his fingers reaching down over my ass.

"You better kiss me before you leave."

He squeezed one cheek hard as he pressed his mouth to mine and kissed me in the hallway, his powerful arms holding me tight, holding me with sexy, manly affection. He breathed into my mouth as he kissed me, parting my lips with perfection, his cologne entering my nose and making me think of the smell on my sheets.

He rubbed his nose against mine before he turned and walked away.

I watched him go, my eyes heavy with fatigue and my heartbeat slow. I needed to get inside and get to work if I was going to hand in that article in the morning, but I stayed there, watching until he was completely gone from my sight.

TWELVE
CHARLIE

I picked up a sandwich on the way home and entered the apartment.

It was quiet because Carson was asleep in her room. She'd dropped off her article in the morning and then immediately went back home since she'd pulled an all-nighter. Sleeping through the day like that should make it impossible to sleep tonight, but she'd done this before, and she had no problem going back to a normal sleep schedule.

I sat at the dining table with my laptop and unwrapped my sandwich.

Her bedroom door opened, and she walked down the hallway in baggy sweatpants and a t-shirt that was several sizes too big. Her makeup was gone, her hair was a mess, and she blinked a few times to adjust to the daylight. "Is that a sandwich…?" She stopped in front of the table and stared at it.

I rolled my eyes and placed one half on a napkin and pushed it toward her seat.

She sat down and ate with me.

I'd purposely gotten the biggest size because I'd anticipated this. Whenever I brought food home, I always halved it with Carson. But I never complained because she was the one who bought the groceries and stocked the kitchen, getting things she knew I liked without asking me to pay for them. It balanced out. "Heard from Vince?"

"No." She took another big bite and chewed it all. "Which isn't a good sign."

"Why?"

"He must still be ripping it apart."

"It's a pretty long article. He's gotta fact-check it and everything."

"Yeah, but there's going to be a lot of shit for me to fix."

"He seemed eager to publish it, so maybe not."

She shrugged and kept eating.

I rubbed my neck and let out a quiet sigh.

She glanced at me. "Stop sleeping on the couch."

"It's too hard to get up. I'm comfortable at the time."

"I'd pick you up, but I'd just drop you again."

"What happened with you and Dax last night?" I wasn't sure if Carson would get annoyed with me for inviting her lover to the apartment, but she'd seemed cool with it.

"We got Chinese food and had sex."

"Cut-and-dried, huh?"

"I mean, we talked and stuff too." She took another big bite, devouring half her portion already. "He actually invited us to join his basketball league on Wednesday nights."

"Really? Where?"

"Somewhere in the city."

"That's cool. I should be able to make that work."

"Invited Matt too. Well, actually, he invited just you and Matt, and I had to inform him that I'm a better player than both of you."

I smiled. "You'll show him on the court."

She finished her half, a pile of crumbs on the napkin underneath her.

"How are things going with him?"

"Fine." She grabbed my glass of water and took a drink.

"Just fine?" I asked. "He's a cool guy."

"Yes." She rolled her eyes. "He's sexy and cool. I realize that. I am the one sleeping with him."

"See anything more happening?"

She shook her head. "Charlie, don't push it."

"What?" I asked innocently. "This is a high-quality guy on your hook right now. Don't throw him back in the water and expect to catch something better."

She took another drink from the water glass.

"And I can tell he's into you."

"We have good chemistry," she said simply.

"No. I mean, I've seen the way he looks at you. I don't think you're just some random woman to him."

"God, I hope not."

I didn't want to get into this territory with her because she was so stubborn, but I wanted her to leave the past in the past and move on. Her walls were so high that a plane couldn't even reach her. "Would it be that terrible?"

"If I'm going to try to be in a relationship again, he's the last guy I'd pick."

"What?" I asked incredulously. "Why?"

"Because he's so sexy and so suave."

I raised an eyebrow, having no idea what that meant.

"Men that beautiful are never around for long. They're always getting offers on the table, and when one becomes too tempting, they either leave you or cheat. Pretty playboys are the worst."

"You know, you're making a lot of assumptions about him."

"You're the one making assumptions." She turned back to me. "I actually know the guy."

"I'm a good-looking guy, and I'm not like that."

She stared at me for a while, her eyebrow raised. "Tell me you're joking."

I stared back, feeling my body tighten in offense. "I'm not like that," I repeated.

"You were in a great relationship with Kat for two years, and then you met Denise, and you jumped ship. Charlie, that's exactly how you are."

That was like a knife right to my windpipe. "That's not how it was—"

"You found someone better, so you left."

"That's not how it happened—"

"You were totally happy with Kat. Your relationship was solid. Denise walks through the door, and then everything changes. If Denise had never moved here, you and Kat would still be together right now. So, yes, that is what happened, Charlie."

I inhaled a deep breath, feeling like shit. "It wasn't like Denise hit on me and I went for it—"

"But you would have—no offense."

"Come on, I'm better than that."

"I'm sure you would have broken up with Kat first, but yeah, you'd jump into bed with Denise." When she saw the sadness on my face, she backed off. "Charlie, I'm not trying to make you feel bad. You aren't a bad guy. But really attractive men are never in one place too long. When they get to their late thirties and realize their looks are fading, they commit. But until then, they're always gonna jump around."

I didn't view the situation in that way, but Carson was right. I'd had a great thing with Kat. She was interesting, funny, beautiful, the sex was great, but I threw it away because Denise caught my attention. If I had been really committed and happy, I wouldn't have paid any attention to Denise. "Maybe Kat wasn't the right person for me."

She turned back to me, her eyebrow raised again. "Charlie, I'm not judging you. You don't need to explain yourself."

"Would I have noticed Denise if I were entirely happy? It's not like I always do that—"

"Kat is the only long-term relationship you've ever really had. And again, it doesn't matter. I'm just saying, someone like Dax, a hot piece of ass who's charming and witty...he'll only be around for so long. He told me he's with models and actresses."

"He said that?" I asked in surprise.

"Well, not like that. I kinda dragged it out of him."

"I still think you're making a big assumption about him."

"It's not about him. It's about men, in general." She eyed the leftovers of my sandwich. "Are you going to eat that?"

I chuckled and pushed it toward her.

"Thanks. I didn't eat breakfast...or lunch." She picked it up and took a bite, not caring about the place where my mouth had been.

I was disappointed that Carson was still so scarred. It'd been a year. But everyone moved at their own pace, and she just needed some time.

WE SHOWED up at the gym and walked into the private room with the court.

Dax was there with a couple guys, their shirts off because they worked up a sweat while on the court.

Matt grinned. "I'm so happy right now."

I chuckled then walked to the bleachers to put down my water bottle.

Carson was in shorts and a black tank top, her long hair slicked back into a ponytail. The second she was there, she attracted the attention of the guys, making them lose their focus on the ball.

Dax was in black shorts that were low on his hips, showing off his fit torso, his powerful shoulders shining under the fluorescent lights because of all the sweat. He had muscular legs too that were tight and lean but dissected by the different muscle groups. When he noticed the disrupted nature of the other men, he glanced at the benches. His expression immediately changed when he spotted Carson, his eyes turning warm, his lips softening into a subtle smile.

Carson was drinking from her water bottle and didn't notice.

Dax called for a break and then joined us, his eyes still on Carson. He stepped closer to her, his hands on his hips, his chest coated with sweat.

She turned to him and looked him up and down. "Damn."

He grinned and leaned down to kiss her.

"Whoa, buddy." She pressed her hand into his chest. "Come on, we're just friends."

His eyes narrowed on her face, irritated by the rejection. Then he circled his arm around her waist and tugged her in anyway, forcing a kiss to her lips.

She didn't fight it this time.

When he pulled away, a gleam of his sweat was around her mouth.

He turned to me next and extended his hand to shake mine. "Glad you guys could join us."

I shook his hand. "Thanks for including us."

Matt looked at the guys on the court. "Thank you. Thank you. Thank you."

Dax chuckled as he shook his hand. "We're pretty competitive. Left with a bloody nose last week. But they'll go easy on Carson."

"I don't need anyone to go easy on me." Carson joined us, her arms crossed over her chest. "I can handle my own out there. Compared to Baghdad, this is a joke."

"What happened with your article, by the way?" Dax asked.

"I turned it in but haven't heard from my boss yet. Not sure if that's a good thing or a bad thing…"

"I'm sure it's fine, sweetheart." He turned back to the court. "We need two players. Who wants to sit out?"

"Oh, I will." Matt took a seat. "I'm happy to be a spectator for this."

"Let's do this." I moved onto the court.

Dax gave Carson's ass a playful smack before he walked away. "I'm covering you."

"Good luck keeping up with me."

"I kept up with you pretty well last night." He winked then jogged onto the court.

CARSON and I were on the same team, so we relied on each other to get the ball across the court because we had a connection, while the rest of the guys were strangers.

Dax stayed on Carson like he said he would, covering her closely, towering over her and giving her a hard time when she tried to pass the ball. And he definitely invaded her space more than necessary, his hands moving to her hips, to her back, touching her and grinning as he did it.

The guys were definitely impressed by Carson's skill. She couldn't run as fast as the rest of the guys, but her shots were good and she had great instincts. She ran to the hoop like she was going to dunk it, making all the guys pause in surprise, but then she threw the ball back to me. I managed to sneak around and make a three-point shot.

At some point, the guards rotated, and some other guy was covering Carson.

"Tim, switch with me." Dax left his guy open to take Carson.

"I got it." Tim kept his arms up, so Carson had nowhere to go. All our teammates were covered, and he suffocated her, tried to get her to drop the ball, moved into her space unnecessarily.

When Carson attempted to take advantage of an open player, she tried to jump up and throw it, but Tim knocked her down.

"What the fuck did I say?" Dax went from calm and suave to psycho in a nanosecond.

"Guys, I'm fine." Carson got up like nothing happened.

Dax glared into Tim's face. "Go."

Tim jogged to the other player.

I knew Dax wasn't being possessive of Carson. He was just concerned she would get hurt, because once the guys realized she was a good player, they would forget she was a chick and treat her like a dude. The best way to ensure she didn't was to guard her himself.

"You alright?" Dax's hand went to her arm.

"I'm fine. Seriously, I've been through worse. He didn't mean anything by it."

Dax let it go, and we resumed the game.

WHEN WE FINISHED, we wiped off with towels and prepared to leave.

"You guys want to get a beer or something?" Dax asked, wiping the towel over his bare torso to collect all the sweat.

"Beer?" I asked. "I'd rather have food. I speak for Carson too."

He chuckled. "Beer and food, it is."

"Thanks for looking after her on the court," I said. "She's tough, but sometimes she doesn't know her own limits."

"Yeah, I've noticed." His smile faded away.

"I know she's difficult, so please don't give up on her."

He lifted his gaze and looked at me again, surprised by what I'd said.

I was equally surprised I'd said it. "She's just got some really thick walls, and it's hard for her to let anybody in. Well, anybody besides us."

"Some guy really fucked her up, huh?"

I shrugged.

"I've been there."

"You have?" I asked in surprise.

He nodded. "I get it." He pressed the towel to his face to pat the sweat from his forehead.

"Does she know that?"

"Yeah."

Then why was she being so difficult? He was the perfect guy to start over with.

Dax moved his hand to my shoulder and gave me a friendly squeeze. "I like that you look after her."

"She's like my sister."

"Yeah, I can see that. We'll see what happens. I really like Carson, but I'm not gonna bend over backward for someone forever. She's either gotta meet me halfway, or I'll move on."

I didn't want Dax to go anywhere. He was the best guy she'd brought around in a really long time. "I'll work on her."

THE FOUR OF us went to a sports bar and got some appetizers and beers.

Dax sat beside Carson in the booth, drinking his beer while glancing at Carson from time to time. "I've got to be honest, sweetheart. When you told me you were good, I wasn't expecting you to be *that* good." He leaned back and slid his arm over the back of the booth.

"Why?" She grabbed a handful of fries and shoved them into her mouth.

He shrugged. "Good is an arbitrary description."

"I told you I played in college."

"But do you play regularly now?"

"No."

"It's natural to get rusty. But you dominated the court like you play every day."

She smiled slightly, clearly touched by his praise.

I drank my beer and kept my mouth shut, but I wanted to tell Carson that he wasn't a man intimidated by a woman's ability, that he was impressed rather than uncomfortable, that he was so secure that he never felt unsure of himself. That wasn't the experience I'd seen Carson have throughout her life, so this was something to hold on to.

"Well, you were good, too." She dunked her fries into the ketchup before putting them in her mouth.

"I can tell the guys were impressed," Dax said. "But then they forgot that you were a girl."

"There's nothing wrong with that," she said.

"Well, I don't want you to get hurt." His hand moved to her other arm. "You're too pretty to get hurt."

She grinned again while looking at her fries. "Too pretty, huh?"

He nodded, looking at her with amusement in his eyes.

She dunked a fry into the ketchup before holding it out to him.

He opened his mouth and let her place it on his tongue before he chewed it.

"Okay, you're hogging the fries." Matt tugged the basket closer to us. "Get some to go and continue that at home."

Carson chuckled. "You're just jealous that Dax is the hottest guy on the planet...and he's mine."

Matt narrowed his eyes. "Bitch."

A smile moved into Dax's expression, but he covered it by drinking from his beer.

THIRTEEN
CARSON

I knocked on the open door. "Lay it on me, Vince."

He looked up from his laptop, then quickly shut it. "We're running it tomorrow."

"What?" I stepped inside and gripped the sides of my skull. "No."

"Yes."

"No revisions?"

"I made a few changes, but other than that, it's solid. Took a while but..."

"That's why it's solid. Because I worked my ass off, alright?"

He grinned. "You always work your ass off, Carson."

I did a little dance in front of his desk, throwing my hands in the air.

He chuckled. "Do that somewhere else."

"So, what am I going to work on next?" I dropped my hands and straightened, becoming professional again.

"Not sure. Take a break."

"Take a break?" I asked incredulously. "This bitch doesn't take a break."

He rolled his eyes. "You've earned a day or two. Enjoy it."

"Alright, fine. But I want something good." I headed out of his office. "Something scandalous."

"Carson?"

I turned back to him, standing just outside his office.

"Good work."

DAX TEXTED me at the end of the day and asked me to join him at the bar for a drink. I walked inside and found him sitting in the booth, drinking his usual scotch, while my glass of Bordeaux sat there, calling my name.

He was looking out the window when I slid into the booth. In a dark t-shirt and with a clean jaw, he was sexy, as usual. He turned his gaze on me, his brown eyes beautiful and deadly, his short hair begging to be fingered. He greeted me silently, taking another drink of his scotch.

"They're running the article tomorrow."

He set down his glass, a soft smile on his lips. "That's great. I'll grab a copy."

"It's a looooong article."

"I'll read every word. Congratulations." He held up his glass.

I tapped my wine against his scotch and took a drink. "Thank you."

"Are you off to the next article?"

"No." I rolled my eyes. "My boss gave me a few days off."

"And that's a bad thing?"

"I'm one of those people who are happiest when they're busy."

"No surprise there." He took another drink before he set the glass down.

I stared at him for a while, feeling my heart start to ache with pain. The breath slowly left my nostrils, a little shaky, a little uncertain. I looked into my glass before I swirled it and brought it to my lips.

His eyes were on me the entire time. "What?"

"What?" I licked my lips.

"You just crashed and burned. What's wrong?"

He could read me as well as Charlie. He was naturally observant. "There's nothing wrong. I just wanted to talk to you about something..."

"Alright." He held the glass in his fingertips, sitting there in a rigid position, so still like a statue. His eyes didn't blink, and his presence suddenly became hostile, as if he already knew what would happen before I said a single word.

"I think we should just be friends."

No reaction at all. He continued to stare at me like he hadn't heard what I said. He still didn't blink.

I took a breath and waited for a reaction.

Still nothing.

"I just think we've had our fun and—"

"Sweetheart, be real with me."

Now I was still because I was surprised by what he said.

"You're ending this with me because you actually like me."

"No. I just—"

"Don't lie to me." He kept his voice low and never raised it. But he could somehow be loud while being quiet.

I shut my mouth.

"You're cutting ties before these feelings grow. Because you're scared—fucking scared."

I took a deep breath but didn't speak. It was the first time I had nothing to say.

"I thought you weren't scared of anything." He lifted his glass and took a drink.

I didn't like being on display, being observed through a lens inside a microscope. I didn't like that he didn't let me get away with things other men didn't even notice. He called me out on my shit, put me in my place, and I hated it...but respected him for it. "I guess I'm scared of one thing..." I inhaled a deep breath, feeling the old pain blossom once again.

His hostility dipped slightly. "What happened, sweetheart? What did this man do to you?"

I shook my head.

"I've got a past too. Show me yours, and I'll show you mine."

I pulled my wine closer and took a drink. "It doesn't matter. It doesn't change my decision—"

"Answer me."

"I was married," I blurted. "Happily married. And he had an affair with his assistant right under my nose, and I didn't even notice…because I trusted him blindly. He left me for her…" I looked into my glass and stared at the wine so I wouldn't have to look at him.

He was quiet.

"It's been a year. Maybe it's been long enough for me to move on, but I'm genuinely not interested in having another relationship. They never work. They never last. People you trust will backstab you at some point. I just don't want to do it anymore." I took a drink, my head still down.

"That's not true. Your friends would never backstab you."

"That's different."

"It's not. You love them and they love you. It's love, sweetheart. That can be applied to a man too. You've just got to find the right one."

"I thought my husband was the right one."

"Well, we all make that mistake."

I lifted my gaze and looked at him, inhaling a deep breath. "You?"

"Pretty much the same story… with just a few differences."

"Really?" I asked in surprise. "You're perfect."

He didn't smile or seem touched by the raw comment. "I think the same thing when I look at you. So, maybe we aren't the problem. Maybe these two people were the problem—and we need to let it go."

"When did this happen?"

"About a year ago."

"Why are you in such a better place than I am?" It'd been the same amount of time, but he was confident and strong.

"I'm not in a better place."

"It seems like you are..."

He stared down into his glass before he shook his head and took a drink. He licked his lips to catch the drop he missed. "Because I understand that it wasn't my fault. That there's nothing wrong with me. She's just not a good person...and I didn't see it at the time. Not because I'm stupid, but because I don't spend my time looking for the bad in people. I'd rather see the good." He grabbed his glass and took another drink.

I inhaled another deep breath, feeling even more connected to him than before. He really was incredible, not just because of his looks, but because of everything underneath that hard chest. This had never happened before, that I'd found a guy I actually liked...and I didn't like that. "I'm just not in that place yet. I'm not ready to even try. I'd like to just be friends...and if you don't want that, I understand." I knew I'd found buried treasure, and I was choosing to cover it up with dirt again. I knew I'd found a stunning diamond, but I was choosing to throw it into the ocean. I looked like a crazy person.

He stared into his glass for a while, his fingers gently spinning it on the surface. He had such sharp features and dark eyes that were impossible to read. He held that position for a long time, processing what I'd said. "Alright." He lifted his gaze and looked at me. "Friends it is."

"WHAT THE FUCK is wrong with you?" Charlie was on my ass the second I walked in the door. "Are you crazy?"

Matt was on the couch. "He's, like, the hottest guy in the world."

"And he's a good guy," Charlie snapped. "Why would you call it off?"

"Stop." I held up my palm, silencing him. "Don't you think it would be worse to see him and waste his time? To try a relationship when my heart isn't totally in it? Yes, I like him, and that's why I'm not going to do that to him. I know what it's like to think you and another person are on the same page, and then to find out you're completely wrong."

Charlie didn't have a response to that because I was right.

"And I can't rush it. I'm not there, alright?"

"I think you could be there if you actually tried," Charlie said. "You like being devoid of all emotion because it's easier that way. It's not because you aren't ready. It's because this is safer."

"Shut up, Charlie," I snapped. "You have no idea what you're talking about."

"You're my best friend. I know *exactly* what I'm talking about. I know you better than you realize because I observe you objectively."

"Look, it's done," I countered. "I already broke it off, and he accepted that."

Charlie moved his hands to his hips, looking at me furiously. "So, what now? You're just gonna hang out as friends?"

"Yes."

"And you think that won't be awkward?" he asked incredulously.

"Not to me. He seemed fine with it."

He rolled his eyes then headed to the couch. "I think you just lost a really great guy, Carson. But whatever. Do whatever you want." He plopped down and grabbed his beer, giving me the cold shoulder.

"Why is this so important to you?" I countered. "I don't need a man to be happy—"

"It's not about having a man." He turned to me. "It's about moving on. It's about accepting something good in your life."

"You don't even know him. He could be a—"

"I read people pretty well, and I think he's the best guy you've ever met. And you just fucking blew it."

FOURTEEN
CARSON

It was all over the news.

Once my article hit the stands and the internet, it was all anyone could talk about.

And I was so proud to have my name listed on the story.

A dream come true.

Colleagues came by my desk and asked me about my process, where I got the information, what it was like to shake down the big banks. It had taken me years to move up in the office, to get these stories, and I was filled with so much pride. It filled the void in my chest, the emptiness that was so deep.

My phone lit up with a text message from Dax.

Good job, sweetheart. There was a picture of the newspaper on his desk, the headline and my name on the front.

I read the message three times, was touched by the words he'd written to me, the fact that he still went and bought the newspaper even though I'd dumped him. It was so sweet I didn't know what to say. My eyes softened, and I grabbed my phone, unsure what to say back, to express how much that meant to me. *Thank you.*

He wrote back instantly. *See you on Wednesday. We'll get a drink to celebrate.*

Alright. See you then.

I WALKED through the door with the bags of groceries in my hands.

Matt and Charlie were getting ready to leave.

"You guys going out for dinner?" I set the bags on the dining table. "Because I got some important stuff, including beer." I lifted a six-pack from the bag and held it up. "The good shit too."

"Dax hooked me up with one of his friends." Matt waggled his eyebrows. "So, we're going out for an introduction."

"Oh, that's great." I turned to Charlie. "Where are you going?"

"Tagging along," Charlie said. "It's casual."

"Oh." I didn't expect Charlie to continue to see Dax so much, but now their friendship was solidified. I didn't mind. I was just surprised.

"You want to come along?" Charlie asked. "They got those fries you like."

"Ooh...I do like fries. And I'm interested to meet this fella for Matt."

"Dax already sent me a pic," Matt said. "And he's hot."

A part of me didn't want to see Dax because it felt too soon, but I also wanted to see his face after that text he'd sent me a few days ago. I glanced at the groceries, knowing I couldn't cook anything decent without Charlie there. "Let me put these away, and we'll go."

Charlie didn't say anything about Dax. After I told him I'd ended things, he let it go. "Hurry up. We're starving."

"For food as well as dick," Matt said.

I put the groceries away, and we walked to the restaurant. When we stepped inside, Dax was sitting there in a classic shirt, his muscular arms stretching the seams. He was listening to his friend talk, a focused expression on his face, his dark eyes sexy.

"Ooh...he's even better in real life," Matt said to Charlie.

"I wonder if he plays basketball," Charlie said back.

"He could play badminton, and I wouldn't care," Matt said with a chuckle.

We walked to the table, and I couldn't believe I'd forgotten how sexy Dax was. He was so gorgeous, so fit, so perfect. I couldn't kiss him the way I used to, greet him in any kind of affectionate way, and now I missed it a little.

Dax turned to us when he heard us approach. "Hey, guys." He rose to his feet, and he hesitated slightly when he realized I was there. His eyes narrowed on my face. The look only lasted a nanosecond, but it was long enough to show a slight hint of affection. He turned back to the guys. "Matt, this is my friend Jeremy."

Jeremy shook his hand. "Pleasure to meet you."

"Pleasure is all mine." Matt shook his hand as he looked him up and down appreciatively.

Charlie leaned into his ear. "Be cool, man."

Jeremy chuckled. "It's flattering. I like what I see too." Jeremy shook Charlie's hand next. "Nice to meet you."

I came closer then shook his hand. "Carson. Nice to meet you."

"Definitely." He glanced at Dax before he looked at me again. "You're gorgeous."

"Oh...thank you." I smiled, loving a compliment from a gay man.

We walked around the table and sat down. Matt sat across from Jeremy, and Charlie sat across from Dax. That left me at the end of the table, but it brought me closer to Dax than if I were sitting across from him.

Matt and Jeremy immediately started talking.

Dax looked at the menu. "I'm not in the mood for beer. I'm getting something stronger."

"Like what?" Charlie asked.

"A scotch."

"Damn." Charlie looked over the menu. "If I drink scotch, I'm down for thirty-six hours."

"True," I said. "I've seen it."

Dax put down his menu and turned to me. "What about you?"

"The cheeseburger."

He raised both eyebrows, a smile rising to his handsome face. "I meant, to drink."

"Oh..." I looked at the menu again. "Probably the blueberry martini. Sorry, I'm just hungry. Didn't eat lunch today."

The waiter came over and took our orders then returned with the drinks.

Matt and Jeremy hit it off right away.

For Dax and me, there was a bit of an awkward pause.

Charlie glanced between us before he took a drink.

Dax turned to me. "I really enjoyed your article."

I knew he wasn't just saying that. He'd read every word. "Thank you. Means a lot to me."

"I understand why it took you so long to put together."

"Nobody wanted to talk, of course. But once you pull out one block, the whole thing becomes unstable, and then more and more people talk to save their necks. But that first block, like in a Jenga set, is the hardest."

He nodded. "I heard the FBI has launched a full investigation."

"They've already made a few arrests, actually. It's the article of my career."

"Some of the biggest scandals have been exposed by investigative journalists before the CIA or FBI even become involved. Like Watergate."

"Exactly." I was surprised he knew that.

"So, you should be really proud of yourself." He held up his glass and prepared to tap it against mine.

I smiled and reciprocated the gesture. "Thank you."

"You're a great writer, by the way."

"Really?"

He nodded. "I can hear your voice when I read it, even though it's not a narrative piece."

"You can hear her attitude, you mean," Charlie teased.

"Definitely," Dax said. "That's what makes the article so good." He brought his scotch to his lips and took a drink. "What's new with you, Charlie?" He shifted the conversation away from me.

But I kept thinking about what he said, stared at his face while he was busy looking at Charlie, feeling the tightness in my stomach, the way my nerves set on fire. I brought my glass to my lips and took a drink, trying to drown my urge with booze.

"Carson is the talk of the office right now, so I'm pretty much invisible," Charlie answered.

"What are you working on?" Dax asked.

"A small piece about this independent movie theater in town that's about to close. It's been surviving on donations because of its historical significance to the city, but it's getting more difficult to stay open. They tried to have it made into a national landmark, but that didn't work."

"The industry is changing so much. With streaming services, it's hard for big theaters to stick around." He swirled his glass as he continued his conversation with Charlie. "What's new with Denise?"

I was surprised Dax asked that.

Charlie shrugged. "Haven't seen her much lately."

"Can I ask you something about that?" Dax asked.

"Sure." Charlie glanced at Matt, who was absorbed in his conversation with his date.

"Why did you feel so strongly for her that you would leave Kat? Was there something specific that happened? Or she just walked in, and you knew?"

Charlie shrugged. "I'm not sure. I just feel like...when we're in a room together, the chemistry is so intense that it completely suffocates me. Kat can be sitting right next to me, and it doesn't change anything. Maybe it's all chemical..." He tapped his fingers against his skull. "Or maybe it's not. I really don't know."

"Well, I've got a good guy who would probably fit well with Kat. Maybe something will happen."

All of my friends were going to be dating Dax's friends pretty soon.

"That'd be great," Charlie said. "If Kat is happy, then I can finally do something about it."

Dax turned to me. "Does Denise have any idea?"

I shrugged. "I've never told her how Charlie feels. She's never brought it up to me either. So, I really don't know."

Charlie took another drink of his beer before he got to his feet. "I'm gonna use the john."

When he was gone, it was just the two of us.

Dax drank his scotch then turned his gaze on me, watching me with his elbows on the table, that focused expression that held a million thoughts inside aimed right at me.

I returned the stare, felt my heart race, felt the numbness in my fingertips.

"Have you and Charlie ever been together?"

An eyebrow almost rose off my face because I was so surprised by the question.

"You guys get along so well together...it seems like a good fit." He brought his glass to his lips and took a drink.

He was my friend now, and friends shared. I had nothing to hide. "Nothing has ever happened between us. We've been friends since we met, and he kinda just got friend-zoned. And we do get along well, but we're also terrible for each other at the same time."

"How is that possible?"

I shrugged. "We butt heads a lot. We disagree on almost everything. And honestly, there's just no attraction there. I think Charlie is a good-looking guy and he's got a nice body, but I've never had the urge to jump his bones. It's weird."

"He's just not your type."

"I guess. I've never been into blonds."

He smiled, probably because he had dark hair that was similar in color to his eyes. His hand grabbed his glass once more, and he brought it to his lips for a drink. "I thought it was sweet that you tucked him in that one night."

"Tucked him in?" I asked.

"On the couch."

"Oh." I chuckled. "I just didn't want him to get cold in the middle of the night, wake up, and stumble to his bedroom and trip along the way."

"Exactly. Sweet." He took another drink.

I'd had guys be jealous of my relationship with Charlie, wondering if we hooked up in secret, if we'd ever been together in the past, and sometimes it was such an obstacle that I had to dump them. Dax seemed curious but not jealous. "Ever slept with a friend?"

He set his glass down and considered my question. "You."

There was something sweet about his answer, but I couldn't identify what it was. "I mean, someone like Charlie. Do you have someone like that?"

He shrugged. "You're the only girlfriend that I have."

"Really?" I asked in surprise.

He nodded. "I guess I have my sister, but that doesn't really count."

"Wow. I feel kinda special."

"You should. I feel like the women in my life have one single purpose. When that purpose is over, our relationship is concluded. But you and I... I feel like we have more than just that physical purpose."

Again, it was sweet. Almost too sweet.

Charlie returned from the bathroom. "Oh, good. Food's here."

The waitress placed the food in front of us before she walked away.

Dax got a salad with grilled salmon on top. He squeezed his lemons onto the lettuce and started to eat.

I felt a little self-conscious about what I'd ordered, a burger and fries.

Without asking, Dax reached over and grabbed a couple fries before placing them in his mouth.

"Uh, excuse me?" I asked playfully.

He grinned back, like he knew I didn't mean it.

Charlie did the same, reaching for a handful.

I smacked his hand away. "Whoa, what the hell?"

"He can have fries, and I can't?" he asked incredulously. "I came home the other day, and you pretty much devoured *my* entire sandwich."

I considered his words for a moment before I pushed the plate closer to him. "Alright...that's fair."

AFTER DINNER, we walked home.

Matt kept talking about how great Jeremy was, what they had in common, how hot he was. When that was over, Charlie addressed me.

"How was it with Dax?"

"What do you mean?" I asked, walking beside him.

"I mean, it's the first time you've seen him since you broke up," Charlie said. "Was that weird?"

"One, we didn't break up. And two, it was totally fine. Not weird at all."

Charlie walked with his hands in his pockets. "Yeah, it seemed like you guys got along pretty well."

"I think choosing to be friends was the best decision I made. Because at some point, it wouldn't have worked out and it might have gotten ugly, but this way...we can be friends." I was deeply attracted to him, missed kissing him, missed hugging him the second I saw him. But those feelings would go away...in time. "I really like being friends."

KAT and I met up together after work, going to a bar close to both of our apartments. She was in a black dress and heels, her hair slicked back into a ponytail with the curled ends hanging down her back.

I'd just left the office, so I was in my stuffy attire, a pencil skirt and a formfitting blouse tucked in. These clothes were professional and flattering to my figure, but once I started to eat too much, I could hardly breathe.

Sometimes I felt like I had to juggle Denise and Kat, like a two-timer. It was awkward to be around them both, when Kat had no idea that Charlie wanted Denise, and Denise had a really gorgeous man on her hook and had no clue. So I tried to see them individually, but we had a lot more fun when it was all three of us.

Kat looked across the bar to another booth. "Isn't that Dax right there?"

I turned to follow her gaze, finding him in a booth with a group of guys, their beers in front of him, a beautiful woman beside him, leaning in close and finding any excuse to touch his arm. There was a bit of jealousy when I looked at the supermodel he'd go home with at the end of the night, but I tried to focus on his face, the way his five-o'clock shadow had grown in and how his eyes lit up when he was having a good time. "Yeah, it is."

"And who's that skank?"

I shrugged and looked away. "None of my business."

"The two of you are really done?" She sipped from her drink, looking at me through thick lashes. She had plump, cherry-colored lips, soft eyes, and a complexion that made her look like a doll. She was gorgeous, so I didn't understand why Charlie had lost interest so abruptly when Denise came around.

"I wouldn't describe it like that. It was just casual."

"Yeah, but it seemed like you were into him."

"I mean, he's super hot…and a good guy." The more I got to know him, the more I realized he was special. He wasn't average in intelligence or appearance. He was thoughtful, observant, secure…perfect. "But we're just friends now."

"And you're okay with that?"

I shrugged. "It's better this way. I'm just not ready for something more."

"Did he want something more?"

"Not explicitly, but I was starting to like him, so…I jumped ship."

She gave me a sad look.

"I'm fine. Really. We were never exclusive, so I don't care if he's with someone else."

She glanced at his booth again but abruptly turned back to me. "Well...he's coming over here."

"He is?" I asked in surprise.

She nodded discreetly before grabbing her drink.

Dax appeared at the table, tall, dark, handsome. His hands were in his front pockets, and his attention was on me. "Hey." His eyes were lit up with affection, and he was friendly, like he wasn't uncomfortable being seen with another woman, a woman much more beautiful than I was.

"Hey." I forced a smile and acted natural.

"Just the two of you?" He was in jeans and a shirt, his muscular body noticeable in the way everything fit him.

"We wanted to get together and talk shit about work," Kat said. "We do it at least once a week."

His gaze shifted to her. "What do you do?"

"Personal shopper for rich people," she said.

"Wow." He nodded. "That sounds interesting."

She shrugged.

He glanced back at his table before he turned to us. "You know, I've got a friend over there that I intended to introduce you to. His name is Nathan."

Kat glanced back to the table. "Which one is he?"

"He's wearing the blue collared shirt."

Kat narrowed her eyes and then clearly liked what she saw because she quickly turned to me. "Ooh...he's hot."

I chuckled. "Go for it."

He nodded to the table. "Come on."

"Oh my god, right now?" Kat asked. "I'm nervous."

"Girl, you gotta go," I said. "Be cool."

"Easy for you to say." She turned back to me. "You took a rifle from an Iraqi soldier and hit him over the head with it."

Dax turned to me, wearing a surprised expression.

"Then this should be nothing." I snapped my fingers. "Get it, girl."

Dax chuckled. "He's harmless. I promise."

Kat took a big drink from her glass then scooted out of the booth. "Wish me luck."

"I don't need to, Kat."

Dax walked her back to the booth and introduced them.

My glass was empty, so I grabbed hers to finish it off. I could walk over there and join them, but I thought it was best to let Kat have all the spotlight. I opened my wallet and pulled out some cash to leave on the table.

Then Dax slid into the booth across from me, scotch in hand.

I stared at him for a few seconds, surprised to see him join me. "What are you doing here?"

"I gave up my seat so Kat could talk to Nathan."

"Oh." I glanced back at the table, seeing Kat talking to the guy she'd been introduced to. The woman Dax had been with stared at our booth, clearly hurt that he'd left her to sit with me. I turned back to him. "The woman you're with seems upset."

He shrugged and took a drink.

"That's it?" I asked in surprise.

"I just met her."

I turned back to him. "Well...she's gorgeous."

"Aren't they all?" He eyed the two glasses in front of me. "Rough day?"

I smiled. "No. Just a dehydrated day."

"Have a new assignment yet?"

"Yeah. Vince gave me a few smaller articles. He wants me to cover the big court case they just moved to Brooklyn. A little below my level, but I'll take it. There aren't very many high-profile articles that come around often."

"So, you've got to tell me about the gun incident."

I rolled my eyes. "Kat made it sound way more intense than it really was."

He gestured with his hand, encouraging me to talk. "Then tell me what happened?"

I shook my head slightly. "I was in the streets of Baghdad, trying to get interviews with people. I had my translator with me. When the soldiers came through, they gave my translator a hard time for helping some stupid American girl. A guy pointed a rifle in his face. I basically took it from him and smacked him upside the head."

Dax had never looked so shocked.

"They left us alone after that."

"Why?" he asked incredulously. "Why didn't they just shoot you?"

I shrugged. "I think they were a little scared of me, honestly."

He shook his head. "I'm surprised you went into that environment with no protection."

"I had a bulletproof vest and a pistol on me. I just didn't reveal it unless I had to."

He shook his head again. "You're a badass chick, you know that?"

I shrugged. "I may have heard that before…once or twice."

A slight smile moved onto his lips.

I noticed the woman rise out of the booth and head for the door. "She's leaving."

He shrugged and kept drinking.

I stared at him in surprise. "You let gorgeous women walk out of your life often?"

That smile was still on his lips. "Not always." He lifted his gaze and looked at me, stared at me without blinking, like his words implied more than they said. "How are you?"

I let the topic drop. "Excited for our game tomorrow."

"Ready to kick some ass?" Without much change of expression, he could show his amusement, his enjoyment when he spoke to me.

"That's all I ever do—kick some ass."

He chuckled. "The guys were really impressed by you. They said you're a great player."

"Well, thanks."

"But I had a talk with them about being too aggressive with you."

I shook my head. "That's unnecessary. If I want to play like one of the boys, I have to be treated like one of the boys. I can handle an elbow to the face or stomach or being knocked on my ass once in a while. Really not a big deal."

"It's a big deal to me." He took another drink then looked out the window.

"Well, that's sweet." I'd never met a man so gorgeous and so kind at the same time. He was easy to talk to, easy to connect with. It was the first time I'd had a conversation with a man that was enjoyable without leading to sex. Just being with him...was fulfilling.

He glanced at his friends at the table. "Looks like they're hitting it off."

I turned when Kat laughed loudly at something Nathan said. "You can join them if you want. I should probably get home anyway."

He turned back to me. "I'd rather talk to you. I see those assholes all the time."

"I feel like you see me all the time too." I'd seen him several times that week, and I'd see him tomorrow night as well.

"Really?" he asked. "I feel like I don't see you enough."

My heart started to ache all over again. Was he purposely making this hard for me? Making me want him even more than I did before?

He spoke again before I could dwell on what he said. "I think they're getting along pretty well." He glanced at Kat again. "Maybe this is the beginning of something."

"Is Nathan a playboy? Just looking for a fling?"

"Not necessarily. If he really likes a woman, he does the relationship thing. So, it just depends on how well he likes her." He took a drink. "You know, not all men are serial playboys only after one thing. There're a lot of guys out there who want monogamy, a deep and meaningful relationship."

"Not the hot ones," I said with a laugh.

He cocked his head slightly.

"Why commit to one woman when you don't have to?" I asked. "Men are all the same."

He swirled his glass, the scotch spinning around. "I respectfully disagree."

"Well, I haven't met one so..."

His eyes narrowed, and he stilled his glass. "You're looking at one."

I released another chuckle, assuming it was a joke. "Come on, Dax. I saw that gorgeous woman all over you, and you ditched her without thinking twice about it."

He was still for a long while, like he needed time to process what I said. "I literally met her five minutes ago. She was our waitress, and when she got off work, she joined us and bought me a drink. Doesn't make me a playboy."

I wasn't sure why we were arguing about this. "Just forget I said anything." I grabbed Kat's glass and took a drink.

"No."

Now I stilled, unnerved by the authority in his tone.

"I was a loving and committed husband in my marriage. I didn't even look at other women. Yes, there were offers left and right, opportunities that never would have made it back to my wife, but I remained faithful because I made a promise. I'm a man of my word. If I say something, I mean it. My fidelity wasn't just based on loyalty and obligation either. I simply didn't want to be with other women. I was happy...at the time."

Now, I felt like shit. "Dax, I'm sorry—"

"I know you've been burned pretty bad. I get it." He raised his hand slightly. "But I'm not him. My boys over there—" he nodded "—they aren't like that either. Not all men are sneaking around in the dark, looking for the next opportunity to be a faithless piece of shit. There are good men out there. I'm one of them. So, I'm not going to sit here and let you stereotype me as some serial pussy-chaser."

Fuck, I'd really messed this up.

"Yes, I fool around, hook up, live the bachelor life. But when I find a woman I really like, I step up." He grabbed his glass and downed the rest of it in a single drink, his eyes furious.

"Look...I'm sorry."

He wouldn't look at me. "I'm going to cut you some slack and forget this conversation happened next time I see you." He turned back to me. "But you need to move the fuck on. You left that piece of shit a year ago, and you're allowing your entire view of the world to be based on one jackass. My wife was a fucking piece of shit who took me for one hell of a ride, but I know not all women are like that." He stared at me, nostrils flared, his eyes darker than before. "I know you aren't like that."

I closed my eyes, feeling lower than dirt.

He slammed his glass down and slid out of the booth. Without saying a word, he walked out and left the bar.

I sat there, feeling like shit, feeling absolutely terrible. I dragged my hands down my chest, felt the pit in my stomach grow, and then forced myself out of the booth to go after him.

The guys and Kat all turned to us, knowing something had happened.

I looked up and down the sidewalk until I saw him, about to cross the street to the next corner. I walked quickly in my heels, not making it through the crosswalk in time and choosing to run the red so I could reach him. "Dax."

He stopped when he heard me. He took a breath before he slowly turned around and looked at me, his eyes still angry. His hands slid into his front pockets, and he stared me down.

I'd been so focused on chasing him down that I didn't know what to say when I finally caught up to him. "I'm really sorry about everything I said. You're right. I was being a jackass. I've been such a jackass since we met. I..." I took a deep breath and let my eyes fall, feeling vulnerable for the first time in a year. "I really, really like you. I haven't—"

His hands slid into my hair as his chest pressed to mine, his mouth landing against mine. In the middle of the sidewalk with people walking by, he kissed me like we were alone in a dark room. His arm wrapped around my back, and he tugged me closer, giving me the best kiss of my life. His masculine hands held me against him, his eager lips made love to mine, and he seized me like I belonged to him.

He pulled away just as quickly as he'd rushed me. "You want me? Then you better fight for me. Because I'm not going to wait around forever, Carson. Either move on from the past and try with me...or I'll move on and all we'll ever be is friends."

FIFTEEN
CARSON

I sat in the armchair in the living room, holding a beer on my thigh even though I hadn't taken a drink. Time passed and the evening grew later, but I stared at the blank TV screen, unsure what to do with myself. I had work to do on my laptop, emails to write, a life to live.

But I was frozen to the spot.

I kept reliving that conversation over and over again.

It made me cringe.

Charlie walked inside, in gym clothes because he must have gone out for a workout. He immediately left his shoes by the door and moved farther into the apartment. "Hey."

"Hey."

He grabbed a water from the fridge then looked at the contents inside. "What do you want for dinner?"

"I'm not hungry."

He quickly shut the door and came toward me. "What's wrong?" he blurted.

I rolled my eyes. "Just because I'm not hungry doesn't mean there's something wrong."

He sat on the couch and looked at me.

"But yeah, there's something wrong."

"Carson, what happened?" He was in his black gym shorts and a t-shirt.

I set the beer on the table and dragged my hands down my face. "I fucked up really bad with Dax."

"What did you do?"

"I ran into him tonight and said some stupid stuff about him being a playboy, all men are playboys, just a lot of stereotypical things, and he got pissed off and stormed off. I went after him, and...he told me I needed to fight for him. Otherwise, he was going to move on."

Charlie stared at me for a while, trying to find the words to say. "I think he has every right to be mad—"

"I know he does. I have been such a bitch since the moment we met."

"I wouldn't say that..."

"It's true. And now I feel really terrible about all of it. Because he seems like such a good guy, too good to be true." I ran my fingers through my hair and sighed. "I have no idea why he likes me. What is there to like?"

"A lot, Carson. You just need to let go of the past and move on."

"I want to...but it's not that easy."

"At least try. Because you don't want to lose this guy."

I shook my head. "No...I really like him."

"And he likes you. He wouldn't have said any of that to you unless he felt that way."

"Yeah."

"So, what are you going to do?"

I grabbed the beer and took a long drink. "Ugh, I don't know. I want to be with him, but I don't think I'm ready for anything serious."

"He's not asking you to marry him, Carson. Just give him a chance."

"Yeah."

"Don't let this guy slip away. He's smart, funny, kind, sexy..."

I turned to him, my eyebrow raised.

"What? He is," he said defensively.

I gave a slight chuckle, feeling a little better. "I'm gonna tell him you said that."

"I don't care. I'm secure in my masculinity."

I smiled. "You're cute."

"Back to the topic of conversation. What are you going to do?"

I shrugged. "I'll talk to him tomorrow...and see what happens."

WE WALKED through the double doors and entered the room with the basketball court. The guys were making shots, passing the ball to take turns. Dax was sweaty and shirtless, drop-dead gorgeous.

Why did I always forget how gorgeous he was?

We put our stuff on the benches. I was in shorts and a tank top, my hair pulled back in a tight ponytail.

Matt hadn't come along because he had work. It was just Charlie and me.

When Dax realized we were there, he left the court and walked to us, his expression hard to read. He moved to Charlie first and shook his hand. "Hey, man. Where's Matt?"

"Got caught up at work," Charlie said.

"It's cool," he said. "We've got enough players." Dax looked at me next, but he was a bit cold. He didn't extend any kind of affection.

Charlie picked up on the hostility and turned away. "I'm gonna go warm up."

Dax continued to stare at me, like he expected me to say something.

Now that we were face-to-face and he was staring me down like that, I lost my confidence and didn't know what to do other than squirm.

When he realized I didn't have anything to say, he gave up and turned away.

"Wait."

He turned back to me, his hands on his hips, a sour look in his eyes.

"I want to give this a chance...if you still want me."

He turned less lethal, his eyes softening subtly.

"Maybe we can talk after the game?"

He continued to stare, holding his silence, his hands on his hips, still irate.

Now I was afraid he'd had a change of heart overnight.

Then he moved into me, his arms circling my lower back, and he pulled me in for a kiss.

I didn't mind the sweat. My arms circled his neck, and I felt the moisture immediately seep into my tank from his bare chest. I kissed him back, grateful for the chance he gave me...when I didn't deserve one.

He pulled away and held my gaze. "Ready to kick some ass?"

I released the breath I was holding, a smile slowly coming onto my lips. The stress suddenly left my body, and I felt free. "Yes...let's do it."

AFTER THE GAME CONCLUDED, everyone said goodbye and started to file out. We patted ourselves dry with our towels and drank from our water bottles. Dax shook hands with all the guys who left.

Then it was just the three of us.

Charlie glanced back and forth between us, trying to read the room.

"Dax and I are gonna get a drink or something," I said, letting him know I was going for it.

"Cool." Charlie smiled then gave me a gentle squeeze on the arm. He turned to Dax. "I know this is gonna come up, so I'd rather you hear it from me..."

I raised an eyebrow.

"I said you were sexy last night. But, like, in a totally straight way."

Dax chuckled. "Thanks for letting me know."

"I know Carson will butcher the story, so I thought I would set the record straight now." He grabbed his water and towel and walked out.

Dax watched him go before he turned back to me. "I think I'd rather hear your version instead."

I smiled as I crossed my arms over my chest. "I was telling him about what happened last night, and he said you were a catch and I couldn't let you slip through my fingers, basically."

"Well, tell him I said he's sexy too. In a totally straight kind of way."

I laughed as I grabbed my stuff. "Alright. I will."

We walked out together and left the gym.

"So, you want to go somewhere and talk?" We were in our gym clothes and sweaty, so stopping by a bar seemed like a bad choice. "Or we can shower at home and meet up somewhere?"

"How about we skip the conversation altogether?"

I stared at him, unsure what that meant.

"You want to have dinner with me tomorrow night? And yes, I'm asking you out on a date." He stared down at me, his towel over his shoulder, like my response to this question was all he needed to know.

"Sure. I'd love to."

His eyes softened in approval. "Wow...that's nice."

I dropped my gaze in embarrassment.

His fingers moved under my chin, and he lifted my gaze. "I'll see you tomorrow, sweetheart." He pressed a gentle kiss to the corner of my mouth and turned away.

"Alright. See you then."

SIXTEEN
CARSON

I got to the restaurant first and sat at the table alone. It was a nice place, with white linens, lit candles, and a small vase of roses on the surface. I was in a black dress with my hair curled. It was easy for me to feel confident because I was a naturally secure person.

But right now, I felt like a wreck.

My heart was pounding, my ears were ringing, and I couldn't stop changing my position because I needed something to do, a way to fidget. I ordered a glass of wine for myself and a scotch for him since he ordered for me whenever we met at the bar.

Then he walked in.

It was the first time he wasn't wearing a tee and jeans. He was in a nice collared shirt that fit his sculpted arms well. It was still good on his chest since his body was so broad. He also wore slacks over his muscled thighs. He looked like a million bucks.

My heart started to race faster.

It'd been so long since a man had made me feel nervous, gave me butterflies. Or maybe it was just that it'd been a long time since I'd allowed a man to make me feel that way. It'd been so long since I was vulnerable. The last time I'd worn my heart on my sleeve was the day I found out about my husband's affair. Then the walls were stacked high…and never came down again.

He smiled as he looked at me, his eyes lighting up in the sexiest way. He came to my chair and leaned down to kiss me, his hand moving to my thigh naturally, giving me a squeeze as he greeted me.

It happened so fast, I barely had time to take it all in. Then it was over, but my flames still burned.

He sat down across from me and grabbed his scotch. "Thanks, sweetheart." He took a drink then licked his lips.

"You're lucky I didn't demolish the bread basket right away."

"You didn't have to wait for me." He opened the cloth and pushed the basket closer to me. "Come on, you aren't the kind of woman to wait for anything, and I like that about you."

He was so charming. It didn't seem like he even needed to try. I grabbed a piece and smeared butter on it.

He took a piece too but skipped the butter. "You look beautiful."

"Thank you." My confidence was weak, and I felt the butterflies grow into fire-breathing dragons. "You do too."

"Tell Charlie I looked sexy."

I chuckled. "Oh, I will."

He took a bite of his bread and chewed as he stared at me, his jaw clean because he'd recently shaved. His brown eyes were lit up with playfulness, like he didn't hold anything against me for all the bumps in the road. He was the kind of man who didn't hold grudges. He just moved on.

He grabbed the menu and took a look. "I should get the salad, but I'm starving. I'm getting the steak."

"I like that a lot better than the salad thing." I looked over the menu.

"Meaning?"

"I want a man who eats." I kept looking at the menu. "You know, because I like to eat."

He chuckled. "Steak it is. What about you?"

"I think I'm gonna get the steak too."

"Good. I like a woman who eats."

I smiled and set down the menu.

The waitress came over, and Dax took charge right away. "My lady and I are ordering the same thing. Two steaks, medium rare." He handed over the menus, and the woman walked away.

"I don't need a man to order for me." My elbows moved to the table, and I folded my hands under my chin, keeping my back straight.

"I know you don't need a man for anything, sweetheart." He ripped off another piece of his bread and took a bite.

I drank my wine as I stared at him, feeling my nerves burn like they were on fire. When I purposely made him mean nothing, it was much easier to be around him. But now that I'd unlocked the door around my heart, I felt vulnerable anytime I was with him. "What did Nathan think of Kat?"

"Come on—church and state."

"Sorry?"

"You know I can't tell you what he said. Conflict of interest."

"Did he say anything bad...?"

"Only good things. But if I tell you anything specific, you'll tell her."

"I will not tell her."

He narrowed his eyes.

"Alright...I might tell her."

He chuckled. "He had nothing but good things to say. That's all I'll give you."

"Good. Because she had nothing but good things to say too."

"Maybe they'll really hit it off."

"You didn't tell him about Charlie, right?" I didn't want Nathan to know about her baggage before he got a chance to know her.

He shook his head. "You told me that in confidence."

"Thank you."

"But it would be nice if it goes somewhere, to help Kat move on. That way, Charlie can actually act on his feelings."

"Yeah..." Even then, I didn't think it would go well.

"The reason why I asked if something ever happened between you guys is because he's so hung up on your sister. You don't look identical, but it's obvious that you're related. Maybe it's a subconscious thing."

I shrugged. "I think we look nothing alike. I mean, she's got that beautiful blond hair and long legs..."

He smiled like I'd said something funny.

"What?"

"You're so sexy, and you have no idea." He grinned as he shook his head. "Man, that's so hot."

"I'm not totally oblivious to my appearance. I know I'm pretty. I'm not gonna play dumb." I was a confident person, could walk up to a guy in a bar and ask him out, but I didn't think I was the most beautiful woman in the world either. "But I think there's a lot of talent out there, and when you compare me to everyone else, I don't stand out as much."

He chuckled like I'd made another joke. "Whatever you say, sweetheart."

"I'm serious."

"Well, you're a perfect ten if you ask me. Why else would I chase you for the last several weeks."

"You didn't chase me."

"Trust me, I did. You kicked me out of your bedroom before my breathing even returned to normal. Didn't care for that. Can't say that's ever happened to me before. But I came back...because it was kind of a turn-on."

I felt my cheeks blush in embarrassment.

He studied my face, watching me try to hide my reaction. "You must have broken a lot of hearts this year."

I rolled my eyes. "No."

"Come on, you did."

I covered my unease while drinking my wine. "Not on purpose."

"It never is." He drank from his scotch glass and returned it to the table, his eyes on me the entire time. "So, tell me something about yourself."

"I feel like all we ever talk about is me. What about you?"

A subtle smile moved over his lips.

"What?"

"You were worth all the work." He took another drink before he answered. "I've traveled a lot, but I've never been to Iraq."

"Where's the most exotic place you've visited?"

"Egypt."

"Really?" I blurted. "Oh my god, so you saw the pyramids?"

He nodded. "They have tours where you can go inside."

"Shut up."

He chuckled. "I can't. It really happened."

"That's so cool. Egypt is one of the most dangerous places in the world to visit. Why were you there?"

"Work."

"What do you do again?" He'd said something about finance, but he hadn't told me what company he worked for or what his job really entailed.

"I work in finance." He gave me the same answer as before, not elaborating.

"But, like, what company? And what does that mean?"

"Clydesdale Software."

I recognized the company. They were a Fortune 500 company that had been around for a few generations. "Cool. So, you work in the finance department?"

"Pretty much." He swirled his glass. "Accounting, stocks, financial planning, all that boring stuff."

"That's not boring. Where did you go to school?"

"NYU."

"Cool. You don't strike me as a financial planner, but I can see it."

"And what do I strike you as?"

"I don't know... Marketing?"

"Why?" he asked with a chuckle.

"Because you're good at selling stuff."

"When have I ever sold you anything?"

"Uh, you sold me you." I drank from my wine. "I never thought I would be sitting here right now, on a date with a guy, being vulnerable for the first time since the day I found out my husband was nailing his assistant, a girl who just celebrated her twenty-first birthday." I slid my glass around on the table.

His smile slowly faded away at my description. "You sold yourself to me long before I sold me to you."

"I don't see how. I was standoffish, selfish, cold..."

"Yes, except the selfish part. You're definitely not a selfish lover."

My eyes dropped immediately, thinking about all the hot sex we used to have, how we fit together so naturally, how we had such incredible chemistry it was unbelievable.

"And I was smitten the second I heard you tell off that asshole. I'd never met a woman like that. The more I got to know you, the more I saw a beautiful fire that kept me warm. I saw a spunky, confident woman who doesn't need a man for anything...and that's really refreshing."

The compliment cut me deep. "You like independent women?"

He shrugged. "Not until I met you."

"I guess that means your wife wasn't that way."

He shook his head. "Nope. Not even slightly."

"Damsel in distress type?"

"Yes. But she was also just not a good person. I can tell you are."

"Really? You don't know me that well."

"But I see how passionate you are for uncovering the truth and sharing it with the world. You risk your life for it because it's so important to you. You have good friends who love you. You've been dealt a bad hand in life, but that didn't stop you from making it on your own. I think you're an incredible person. That was why I worked so hard just to get a damn date with you." He smiled, telling me he was teasing me.

It made me smile.

"Oh, and you're sexy." He grinned.

"That makes me a good person?" I asked with a laugh.

"No...but it doesn't hurt."

WHEN DINNER WAS FINISHED, the tab arrived, and Dax immediately slipped his card inside.

I grabbed my wallet. "Let's split it."

He leaned his head back and sighed loudly. "Let's not do the check dance."

"Come on. It was expensive." I grabbed the folder.

He snatched it out of my hand. "No."

"I thought you liked an independent woman?" I fanned my card.

"Yes. But I also like taking you out."

"If we have a second date—"

"*If?*" he asked. "Come on, you're totally into me." He smiled, his beautiful eyes playful.

I couldn't control the smirk that spread across my face. "The cost of dates adds up."

"Sweetheart, don't worry about it." He put the tab at the edge of the table.

"This is the twenty-first century. Women pay for shit."

"I'll let you get something sometime. But not tonight. So put that damn card away." He lifted the tab and handed it to the waitress.

I gave up and returned my card to my wallet. "Well...thank you."

He nodded. "You're welcome, sweetheart."

I loved the way he called me that, but I wondered if he called other women that, if it was just a nickname he threw around. But I didn't ask because I didn't want to offend him. "So, what do you want to do now?"

"You want to get some ice cream?"

I loved ice cream, but I hadn't expected him to suggest that. "I was thinking sex at your apartment, but we can do that too."

He leaned farther over the table, his eyes focused on my face. "I like your idea better."

I grinned. "Got any roommates?"

"I live alone."

"Ooh...we could have sex on the couch."

He nodded slowly. "Or the kitchen table."

"Against the fridge."

A subtle smile crested his lips. "You're such a tease."

"No. We can do all of those things."

"But I've got to get there first...and it's pretty difficult to walk when you've got a hard dick in your slacks."

"Then let's duck into an alleyway. That was pretty fun."

He inhaled a deep breath, his eyes darkening at my words, like I was driving him crazy. "Sweetheart...you really are the perfect woman."

SEVENTEEN
CARSON

He unlocked the door then stepped into his apartment.

It had a decent living room, kitchen, and the hallway made it seem like it had two bedrooms. The place was simple, with couches facing a TV on the wall, but most of it was bare, with no decorations or pictures.

He was a bachelor guy living alone, so it wasn't that surprising. His wife probably kept everything in the divorce, so he had to start over. "It's nice."

"You want something to drink?" He set his wallet and phone on the counter and opened the fridge. "I've got beer."

I looked past his shoulder and saw that his fridge was completely empty. The only thing inside was a six-pack of beer. He didn't have any groceries? Did he eat out all the time? I didn't judge him. I was just surprised. He was so fit that I assumed he had a disciplined diet of egg whites and spinach. "Sure."

He twisted off the cap then came back to me.

I grabbed the bottle and took a drink. "You like living alone?"

"Yeah." He looked at me as he lifted his beer and took a drink.

"I'd like to live alone someday, but I've been with Charlie so long that I think I'd probably hate it."

"I think he'd hate it too."

A laugh came from my lips. "He'd love to ditch me. I eat all his food, leave dishes in the sink, come home late—"

"Buy the groceries, tuck him in at night, keep his secret from your best friend and sister. Come on, he loves you."

My eyes softened. "What does he say about me when I'm not around?"

"Nothing but good things." He took a drink from his beer before he walked to the couch. He grabbed the remote and turned on the game.

I sat beside him, holding my beer on my thigh.

His arm moved around me, and he pulled me close, his eyes on the screen.

I should take it as a compliment that he didn't want to jump into bed right away, that he wanted to spend time with me, but I'd been eager since the start of our date, been eager since the last time I'd had him.

I put my beer on the table then pulled his belt through the loops.

He turned his gaze on me, his brown eyes dark and seductive, his lips slightly parted.

I undid the button and zipper then tugged down.

He lifted his hips so I could get his pants off, revealing the hard dick that was trapped inside his clothes. Instead of grabbing me and taking me, he just watched me, as if seeing me take control was sexy.

I got on my hands and knees on the couch then went down on him, my ass in the air.

He sucked in a deep breath through his teeth, his hand immediately moving to my ass and fingering my black thong.

I pushed him to the back of my throat before I placed a kiss on his crown. "Thank you for dinner…"

He leaned his head back and released a suppressed moan, like he couldn't do anything except enjoy it.

MY ARMS WERE around his neck, my fingers deep in his hair, and I held his face close to mine as I kissed him, as I panted and moaned into his mouth while he pleased me, gave me everything I'd given him on the couch.

His bedroom was bare, with the exception of a dresser and a TV. He had a closet, but the door was shut. He had his own master bathroom, but that door was closed too. It seemed like he'd just moved in even though he must have been there for a year.

He rocked into me, rubbing my clit with his body, making me come around his big dick over and over.

God, it was so good. "I missed you…"

He pulled his lips away so he could look at me while he fucked me, his jaw tight, his eyes focused. He thrust his hips and slid deep inside me every time, moving perfectly to where it was easy to forget there was a condom separating us.

My nails started to claw his back, and my knees squeezed his waist. I breathed so hard it seemed like I was hyperventilating, but when I reached the threshold, I came all over him…again. My nails dug deeper, and I moaned loudly, my lips quivering, my eyes wet. Seeing the desire in his eyes as he watched me only turned me on more, made me whimper louder. "Dax…" The sex was better than it was before. Now that I could lower my walls and really let him in, everything was heightened, painfully potent. I could really feel every single sensation on a deeper level.

He moaned quietly as he finished, giving me all his length as he filled the condom, his deep-brown eyes on me, possessive, sexy, dark. He twitched inside me and slowed down his thrusts, his eyes closing for a moment as he finished. Then he leaned down and gave me a final kiss, a gentle massage of my lips.

"That was so good…"

He kissed my neck before he got off me and cleaned up in the bathroom.

Now I wished we were at my apartment so I could just go to sleep. But I had to walk back a couple blocks, half asleep and high off the good chemicals he put into my brain. I turned over and pulled the sheets over my shoulder and closed my eyes. His bed was just a mattress right on the floor. He didn't even have a bed frame. But I didn't care. It was still comfy.

He came back a few minutes later and got into bed behind me, his naked body spooning mine. His chest was hard and warm, and his arm slid over my stomach and his hand rested on my belly button.

"This is the most comfortable bed I've ever slept on."

He pressed a kiss to my neck. "That can't be right."

"Well, after making me come so many times, I'd be happy to sleep on concrete."

When he chuckled, his breath sprinkled across his neck. "I know my place isn't very nice..."

"But it includes you, so it's perfect." I angled my head over my shoulder and pressed a kiss to his mouth.

He stilled at the affection, his eyes on me, his entire body motionless. He stared at my mouth for a second before he kissed me again, this time giving me a deeper kiss, one that lingered.

I lay down again and got comfortable.

His face pressed into the back of my neck. "You're welcome to sleep over."

"I really don't want to walk home right now, but I don't want to have to get up early either. Hmm..."

"Tough decision. But just so you know, I'm not gonna kick you out."

I smiled. "Okay, I deserved that."

He gave my ass a playful squeeze. "I'm never gonna stop teasing you for that."

"I had a feeling…"

"Well, let me know if you want to leave in the next ten minutes. Otherwise, I'm going to sleep…and don't try to wake me up. It won't work."

"Hard sleeper, huh?"

"Like a bear." He inhaled a last deep breath then went still, his arm around my waist, his nose in my hair.

I lay there, trying to come to a decision. I thought it was more appropriate to leave, but I'd kicked him out of my apartment so many times, and if I was trying to be different, I needed to make an effort. I needed to try new things. "I'm going to stay."

He tugged me a little closer, his lips resting against my skin. He didn't have a problem cuddling, didn't have a problem sharing his space. He shared himself with me completely.

I should do the same.

MY ALARM WENT off on my phone the next morning.

"Ugh." My hand reached out to the floor, searching over the carpet to find the thing that was ringing loudly. I had to reach farther to get it, moving away from Dax, who was still in the same position as last night. My eyes were closed, and I groaned as I kept searching for it. When I finally got it, it slipped through my fingertips. "You motherfucker." I grabbed it again, squinted, and finally turned the noise off.

"You fucking cunt." I dropped it back on the carpet and sighed.

He chuckled quietly, his voice raspy. "Not a morning person, huh?"

"Not a cunt kind of person." I turned over onto my back and ran my fingers through my hair, seeing the two of us close together on one side of the bed, leaving the other half empty. The morning light poked through the blinds on the window, highlighting his sculpted physique in the dark, the lines between his various triceps, the distinctive line between his pecs.

"She's just doing her job."

"Well, she's a cunt anyway."

He moved over me and sprinkled kisses along my collarbone, my neck, the valley between my tits. "Is this better?"

With my eyes closed, I nodded. My arms wrapped around his shoulders, and I held him tight. When he came closer, I felt his hard dick against me, rubbing against my stomach, the moisture oozing from his tip.

He moved farther down, over my flat stomach to my hips, his face disappearing under the sheets.

I just lay there and enjoyed it.

Then my alarm went off...again.

He stilled before pulling the blanket off.

"What a fucking bitch." I reached for the phone on the floor again.

"You must have put it on snooze."

"Whatever." I grabbed the phone and stabbed my finger into the screen before I turned it off altogether. "Damn cockblock. Can't you see I'm trying to get laid right now?" I threw the phone down again.

He moved back on top of me. "Sweetheart, you don't have to *try* to get laid." His mouth moved to my neck, and he kissed me again, this time smothering me, pressing me into the mattress. "Because nothing is going to keep me away from you."

THE BATHROOM WAS JUST as stark as the rest of the house. I did my business, washed my hands and face, brushed my teeth with some toothpaste on my finger, and then returned to the bedroom.

He stood in his closet, which only had a couple articles of clothing inside. He grabbed a few things and started to get dressed. He didn't shave or do his hair. He only brushed his teeth. He still looked incredible, but with that messy hair, he didn't exactly look ready for the office.

"Did you recently move here?"

He sat at the edge of the bed and put on his shoes. "No. Why?"

"You just don't have a lot of stuff." I sat beside him, slipping on my heels.

He shrugged. "I'm a minimalist kind of guy."

"I just figured your wife took everything in the divorce."

He rose to his feet then grabbed his phone. "Yeah, that didn't help."

When I was ready, we left his apartment and headed to the street.

"I'm running late, so I'm going to grab a cab." I raised my hand, and immediately, a yellow taxi pulled over.

"Alright, sweetheart." His arm circled my waist, and he gave me a quick kiss. "See you later."

I watched him turn away before I got into the cab. "See you later."

EIGHTEEN
CHARLIE

"Why was it weird?" I sat across from Carson at the bar because we'd decided to get a drink after work.

"I can't explain it..." She held on to her wineglass as she searched for the best way to describe it. "It just seemed like he didn't have anything. The apartment was really empty. There was nothing in his fridge..."

"He's a bachelor. It's not that surprising."

"You're a bachelor."

"But he was married. Maybe he's still used to having a wife, so he doesn't know how to shop for groceries and pick out furniture, you know?"

"Maybe...but he seems pretty independent."

I shrugged and took another drink. "He's only been divorced for a year. He's starting his life over."

"I get that. But... I don't know."

"And maybe he has a ton of student loan payments or something. Old medical bills. Maybe he just can't afford to furnish his place."

"That's fine if that's the case, but then he shouldn't be taking me out for a hundred-dollar dinner." She swirled her glass and watched the wine spin in a circular motion.

"He was trying to impress you."

"An expensive meal doesn't impress me. And a man like that doesn't need to do *anything* to impress me."

I drank my beer again, not alarmed by what Carson was telling me.

"And he didn't have any clothes. He had, like, a couple shirts in his closet and a few jeans."

"His wife threw them away," I reasoned. "Isn't that the cliché? Throwing his clothes out the window and onto the street?"

"But she's the one who cheated—unless that's a lie."

I knew it was Carson's nature to pick at things until she got to the truth. That was just how she was. It was why she was such a good investigative journalist. She found plot holes and kept poking until the lies unraveled. "Give him the benefit of the doubt, alright?"

"I am—"

"Don't blow this by assuming he's a liar."

"I'm not assuming anything. I just know there's something off... I can feel it."

"Maybe you're overthinking it. Maybe he lost a lot of money in the divorce. He's broke now. Maybe he had to sell some of his clothes. Who knows? You just made progress with this guy. Don't fuck it up by poking and prodding. Who cares if he's poor?"

She sighed. "I couldn't care less if he's poor. That's not the issue."

"I would let it go."

She stared into her glass for a while, still swirling. "Here's another thing—"

"Oh Jesus..."

"No, listen." She held up her hand to silence me. "I put on the dress I wore the night before, because I didn't have anything else. I went to my apartment to get ready for work."

"And...?"

"He just threw on a t-shirt and jeans."

I still wasn't following. "And...?"

"There's no way he wears a t-shirt and jeans to work."

"I mean, that's not that crazy—"

"He's a financial advisor for Clydesdale Software. I'm sure he doesn't dress that way at work."

That was a valid point. "Huh. Maybe he went to get breakfast?"

"And he didn't do his hair or anything. He just brushed his teeth."

"Maybe he's off today."

"On a weekday?" she asked incredulously.

"Or he goes in late, and he was going to go back and fix himself up?"

"But do you see what I mean?" she pressed. "Something feels off, and I can't figure out what it is."

I didn't believe Dax was a bad guy, and if he was hiding something, it was harmless. "Maybe you're right. But you need to give him the benefit of the doubt. You're starting over, and that means trusting people until they give you a reason not to."

"Well, he's kinda giving me a reason not to. Maybe I can look—"

"No." I already knew where she was going with this.

She sighed. "Yeah, you're right. I can't do that."

"I'm sure whatever he's hiding is personal. And if you're wrong, you're going to sabotage this relationship. Maybe he got fired, and he's in between jobs. Maybe he doesn't even work at that company."

She cocked an eyebrow. "And you think that's not alarming? I don't want to be with a guy who lies to me."

"I'm just saying, give him the benefit of the doubt."

She grabbed her phone and opened her social media apps.

"What are you doing?"

"Looking him up. See what I find."

"I already asked him. He doesn't do social media."

She set her phone down and lifted her chin, her eyebrow raised. "The only people who say that are over sixty-five."

I shrugged. "Maybe he just doesn't need the validation of his peers over everything little thing he does."

She grabbed her wine again, visibly tense.

"Don't jump to conclusions. Just give this a chance. Keep an open mind. Trust him."

She took a deep breath and let it out slowly. "You know how hard that is for me. All the clues of infidelity were right in front of me, but I blindly trusted him and ignored every one of those signs—"

"Not the same situation, alright?"

She took another deep breath.

"Think about what we do know about Dax. He's a great guy. Don't focus on all these little things. And honestly, you just started to date. You can't expect him to show all his cards, just as he wouldn't expect you to show all yours."

She stared at me, still resistant, but at least listening to me. "I do really like him..."

"I do too. Just let this go. Give it time."

She grabbed her glass and took a drink. "Alright. I'll give it time." She set the glass down and scooted to the edge of the booth. "I'm going to take a piss."

"Such a lady..."

She left, and I drank alone, looking out the window.

A moment later, the voice that echoed in my mind reached my ears. "Hey."

I turned, seeing Denise with her purse strap across her chest, her blond hair in curls. "Hey." I cleared my throat, my heart suddenly racing because her appearance was so unexpected. Carson didn't tell me she would be joining us.

She scooted into the booth and helped herself to Carson's wine.

"I can get you something at the bar."

"No thanks. I already told the waitress. She'll be out any minute." She sat across from me, wearing a pretty summer dress. Her lips were painted red and her eyelashes were thick. She had a softer voice than Carson, because she was softer in every aspect.

"How are you?" I never knew how to talk to her. She made me nervous, which was a first. Women never made me nervous. I could make jokes, carry on a conversation, be charming. But all that went out the window with Denise.

"Good. Had a long shift last night, so I slept in pretty late."

"How'd that go?"

"We were slammed," she said. "There was a pretty bad accident with a lot of casualties."

"That's terrible."

She shrugged. "I'm used to it. But there are times when it gets to me." She turned to the waitress when she brought her cosmo. "Thanks, honey." She placed Carson's drink to the side then drank from her glass. "What's up with you?"

It'd been months since I'd met Denise, and I was afraid I already waited too long. She probably saw me as a friend at this point. But I couldn't just go for it and hurt Kat. We hadn't been broken up very long, and it would just be awkward for her if Denise and I started seeing each other. I'd already tried to forget about Denise by seeing other girls, but it never worked. Sometimes I thought about asking her out in the hope she would reject me and I would have closure to move on. But it seemed pretty weird to ask out someone and hope it wouldn't work out. Very disingenuous. "Carson was telling me about Dax."

"Oh good. She's seeing that hunk again."

"Yeah. But she's getting a weird vibe from him."

"In what way?" She took a sip then licked her lips when she was finished.

Ugh. I hated watching her drink or eat. Fucking distracting. "His apartment is pretty bare, it didn't seem like he was going to work today, stuff like that."

"Sounds a bit shady..."

"I think Dax deserves the benefit of the doubt. I've been hanging out with him a lot, and he seems like a good guy."

"But what do you really know about him?"

"Well, he's got a lot of friends. Assholes don't have a lot of friends."

She gave a loud laugh. "My high school bully was the most popular bitch on that campus. Your assumption is false."

"Guess that's true. But I still think Dax is a good guy."

"Can't you look into him?"

I shook my head. "I don't want Carson to sabotage this relationship before it even starts."

"But I don't want my sister to get hurt again. Getting punked twice in a row...she would never recover."

I didn't want her to get hurt either. She was like a sister to me. I'd do anything for her. "I think she should give it more time."

She drank from her glass again. "Yeah, let's hope for the best."

I drank from my beer and looked out the window so I wouldn't stare at her too much.

"Kat told me she really likes Nathan. I guess they have a lot in common."

I turned back to her. "Oh, that's great."

She grabbed her cocktail straw and stirred her drink. "Is that weird for you?"

I shook my head. "Not at all. It's good that she's getting out there. She's a great girl. Anyone would be lucky to have her." There was nothing wrong with Kat. She was perfect... until Denise walked in.

"It seems like you're totally over her. But I guess that makes sense...since you were the one who ended it."

"Yeah, I've moved on." I didn't want to be harsh toward Kat, but when Denise put me on the spot like this, I wanted her to know there was no attachment to my ex, that I was completely unencumbered.

"What happened?" Denise asked. "If you don't mind me asking. When Kat told me about it, she said it was sudden."

Did she really have no idea? I admired Carson for keeping her word and not sharing my secret. It was a strong sign of loyalty, to lie to her sister and her best friend. It really put her in a tough spot, to have Kat share her feelings, while Carson didn't say a thing. "I just realized she wasn't the right person for me, and I didn't want to waste her time anymore."

She nodded. "That must have been hard, but you did the right thing. Better than being in a relationship when your heart isn't really in it. That's worse, if you ask me."

"Yeah..."

Carson returned from the bathroom. "Hey, girl." She hugged her sister before she took a seat. Then she stared at her drink, her eyebrow raised. "Hmm, that's not my lipstick." She turned to her sister, giving her a look full of accusation.

Denise rolled her eyes and pushed her cosmo to Carson.

Carson grabbed it and took a drink. "That's right, bitch."

I WALKED into the bar with Matt.

"Ooh, he looks good in black."

I eyed Jeremy. "Yeah...sure."

"Sorry, I forgot you only have the hots for Dax." He gave me a playful nudge in the side as he moved forward.

I rolled my eyes.

Dax was there, sitting at the table with his typical scotch.

When we approached, they all got up and greeted us.

I shook Dax's hand. "Hey, man."

He patted me on the back. "Am I the best matchmaker ever? I've got Matt and Jeremy giggling like schoolgirls, and Kat and Nathan seem to really like each other."

"And you and Carson?"

He grinned. "I don't kiss and tell...but that woman's got it bad for me."

I chuckled, knowing he was joking. "I'm glad you guys worked it out."

"She's rough around the edges, isn't she?" He crossed his arms over his chest. "But I wore her down. Got her to sleep over the other night."

"Yeah, she told me. It seems like you've got it bad for her."

He shrugged. "Well, I'm not a chaser. That tells you everything you need to know."

I was tempted to ask him about Carson's suspicions, but I kept it bottled inside. He was charming and easy to talk to, so he seemed completely harmless. It seemed unlikely that he had anything to hide, that he wasn't what he seemed. He probably just had personal issues, and those issues were no one's business.

NINETEEN

CARSON

I sat at the dining table, working on my articles, when Charlie walked inside.

He had a pizza under his arm.

"Oh, you're my hero."

He grinned as he came farther inside, revealing Dax behind him a moment later.

"I was hoping I was your hero, sweetheart." He walked inside, all confident and tall, looking at me with affection in his eyes. He was in jeans that hung low on his hips, a t-shirt that showed off his sexy muscles, and that sexy shadow was along his jawline.

"Well, food takes priority over sex."

Charlie set the pizza on the table. "Don't take it personally, man." He walked into the kitchen to grab plates.

His smile didn't drop, and he leaned over to kiss me in the chair, greeting me like I was his woman and he was my man.

He even slid his fingers into my hair, giving me a hot kiss with no regard to Charlie in the kitchen.

I melted like a grilled cheese sandwich in a hot pan. No man ever kissed me that way, lit my fuse on fire with only his heat. His lips were so good at those delicate kisses, even better at the passionate ones. His hand slid out of my hair as he pulled away.

I was knocked off my feet.

Charlie handed him a plate. "We got half combination and half pepperoni."

Instead of making a comment, I just sat there.

Charlie raised an eyebrow as he looked at me.

"Sorry." I shook my head. "Mind was in the gutter…"

Dax took the seat beside me, a slight smile on his lips.

Charlie turned on the TV, changed the channel to the game, and then joined us.

I shut my laptop and pulled a slice onto my plate.

"What are you working on, sweetheart?" Dax asked.

"A couple articles," I said. "Nothing as exciting as the last one."

"Did you tell him about the FBI?" Charlie asked before he took a bite.

We hadn't talked in a couple days because I wanted to play it cool, so I hadn't mentioned it.

"FBI?" Dax finished chewing his bite and stared at me.

"They came to the office with a subpoena," I said. "Asked me to turn over all my files. I'm also a witness in their investigation."

"Wow," Dax said. "Is that good or bad?"

"Good or bad?" I asked. "It's awesome. I get to testify in court."

"And that doesn't scare the shit out of you?" he asked incredulously.

"Why? I've got nothing to hide. I did my due diligence, fact-checked everything, and these assholes took money from good people. I'm taking them down." I picked up a slice and prepared to put the end in my mouth.

He grabbed my wrist and pulled my hand away as he leaned into me. His mouth was on mine a second later, his fingers sliding into my hair, giving me a purposeful kiss that lasted a few seconds. He pulled back and gave me a soft smile.

Charlie looked away, staring at the TV so he wouldn't have to see our affection.

"What was that for?"

He turned back to his pizza. "Because you're fucking hot."

WHEN THE GAME WAS OVER, Charlie grabbed the empty pizza box and headed to the door. "I'm gonna toss this." He walked out.

Dax was beside me on the couch, his arm over the back of the cushions, his fingertips lightly pressing against the back of my neck. They slowly slid into my hair, gently touching me as he watched the commercial. "So, gonna invite me to stay, or should I take off?"

"You think I'm gonna let you leave without servicing me?"

"Servicing you?" He turned to me, a handsome grin on his face.

"Yeah. That's your job."

"Best job I've ever had."

Charlie returned and cleaned up the plates at the dining table. He left them in the sink. "I'm going to bed. See you later." He walked down the hallway into his bedroom.

Dax kept his stare on me, his fingers still moving on the back of my neck. "I've got one condition."

"I think I already know what it is..."

"Yeah?"

"You get to sleep over?"

He gave a slight nod. "You're quick."

"Of course you can."

"Good."

I turned off the TV and the lights, and we went into my bedroom, which was across the hall from Charlie's.

He walked inside and pulled his shirt over his head. "This is what I don't understand."

My eyes immediately went to his hard body. His beautiful, gorgeous, perfect, hard body.

"How does a straight guy live with a gorgeous woman like you and not lose his goddamn mind?" He grabbed my top and lifted it over my head before his fingers dug into my hair, cradling my head, possessing me entirely now that we were behind closed doors. He stared at my lips as he waited for a response.

"He doesn't think I'm gorgeous." My hands went to the top of his jeans and got them undone.

"Then there's something wrong with him because you are fucking perfect." He tugged my jeans down and gripped my ass cheeks with his large hands, squeezing them hard, handling me roughly, breathing hard, kissing my neck, backing me up to the bed.

My head tilted back, and I was instantly swept away in the heat, immediately drowning in his testosterone. I pushed his bottoms down and felt mine fall, kissing him and panting like we'd been at it for hours rather than seconds.

His hands guided me, gripping me tightly before turning me around and making me face the bed. His arms locked around my body, squeezing me like an animal, his breath heavy on my throat, loud in my ear. "You hear me? Fucking perfect." He grabbed the back of my neck and forced my face down onto the bed.

I got on my knees with my ass in the air, listening to him help himself to my nightstand and grab a condom. He ripped through one, rolled it on, and then thrust inside me like a conqueror breaking down a door to demolish a civilization.

"Fuck..." I gripped the sheets on my bed and let out a moan at his harsh intrusion.

He pounded into me ruthlessly right away, making my bed shake so hard it sounded like it would fall apart any second. His hand returned to my neck, and he pinned me down while he shoved his entire length inside me over and over. "I know you can handle it, sweetheart."

HE LAY on his back with his hand behind his head, his eyes closed and his breathing slow and even.

I was exhausted even though I didn't do anything besides lay there.

He did all the work—and didn't seem to mind. "This is a nice change."

"You're never going to let that go, are you?"

"Nope." He turned his head to look at me, a smile on his lips. "Your bed is pretty comfy."

"Thanks. IKEA."

He faced the ceiling again, closing his eyes with the sheets around his waist.

I hugged his middle and rested my face against his shoulder, smelling his cologne, his body soap, the remnants of his sweat.

He grinned. "I love it when you're all over me."

"I'm *not* all over you."

"Sure, sweetheart."

My phone vibrated on the nightstand, casting the bedroom in blue light.

His eyes opened.

I reached over him and grabbed the phone.

It was Boy Toy #1. *Haven't heard from you in a while.*

I was too tired to respond to this right now, so I put it on do not disturb and returned it to the nightstand.

Dax didn't say anything. If he'd read the screen, he didn't acknowledge it. Then he reached for his own phone and typed a message...to me.

My phone lit up again.

Boy Toy #2: ?

He stared at the phone, seeing the name I had entered in my phone to describe him.

The blood drained from my face, and the fear struck me.

He grabbed my phone, stared at it for a while, and then handed it to me. He didn't say a word, just stared me down, his gaze full of hostility. He could say so much while saying nothing at all.

I took it, my heart beating so fast.

There was disappointment in his eyes, a potent amount. "Change that. Now."

"I put it in that way when we first met—"

"Just change it."

I changed his name to Dax then locked the screen.

He grabbed it and returned it to the nightstand.

We'd come so far, and then I'd fucked it up again with my insensitivity.

He closed his eyes, like he was prepared to go to sleep despite the awkwardness.

I thought he might get up and leave. "I'm sorry…"

He opened his eyes and looked at me again. "It's alright."

I was relieved this hadn't resulted in him storming out and slamming the door in my face. He was clearly angry about it, but not enough to jeopardize our relationship. And he didn't seem to care about the fact that I had another guy on my leash…or maybe that wasn't the priority at the time.

"I don't put Booty #1 and Booty #2 in my phone. You know how offensive that is?"

"Yes, but I'm not the same person anymore."

"I know. That's why I'm going to let this go." He grabbed my arm and lowered me back into him, holding me close, his chin resting on the top of my head. His fingers moved into my hair, and he inhaled deeply as he held me, his powerful chest rising and lifting me with every breath he took.

"Thanks."

He pressed a kiss to my hairline, his body language different now, gentle once more.

And then everything felt alright.

"YOU STILL HAD Boy Toy in your phone?" Kat asked incredulously, standing beside me at the table in the bar. She was in a purple dress, pastel in tone, and her hair was pulled back in a tight ponytail.

"Yeah…"

She cringed. "That's not good."

"I just totally forgot about it."

"Even though it said Boy Toy #2 every time? What did he say about Brian texting you?"

"Nothing. Didn't seem to care about that."

"Are you still seeing him?"

"I haven't talked to him, actually." Once Dax came into my life, he shook up everything, became the primary focus, in good ways and bad ways. I didn't have time to see anyone else, and I didn't even want to see anyone else. Dax was the best lover I'd ever had. Why would I want someone else?

"Are you going to call it off?"

"Probably."

"So, you and Dax exclusive?"

"We haven't said that. But if I'm really giving this relationship a try, it seems disingenuous to sleep with other men at the same time."

"Well, is he sleeping with other women?"

I shook my head. "I haven't asked."

"Before you bend over backward for this guy, maybe you should find out if he's doing all this for you." She grabbed her glass by the stem and took a drink.

He didn't seem to care that Brian texted me, but that could be for any reason. Brian had said he hadn't heard from me in a long time, and maybe that was why it didn't bother Dax. "How are things with Nathan?"

"Great. He's so sexy and funny... I really like him. Matt really likes Jeremy, so Dax is some kind of cupid."

I chuckled. "Seems like it."

"We're going out to dinner tomorrow night."

"Have you done the deed?"

"Not yet, but I'm trying to take it slow. He'll be the first guy since Charlie..."

"And how do you feel about that?" I was in a really awkward position because of this love triangle. It was painful to deceive my best friend, not to tell her the entire truth about Charlie. But I reminded myself it would only make it worse, only be cruel.

She shrugged. "I've got to move on. And Nathan seems great, so..."

"Yeah."

"And he's super hot."

I nodded.

"Charlie and I are never going to get back together, so I've got to push forward." She drank from her glass then turned back to me. "Unless he ever talks about me...?"

This was so painful, to watch her want Charlie, still love him, and I knew he was hard up for Denise. "No...not really." But I couldn't give her false hope. I had to put her on the right track.

She nodded slightly, her eyes filled with disappointment. "That makes sense."

"But Nathan is way hotter than Charlie, so this is way better anyway."

She chuckled. "You think everyone is hotter than Charlie."

"Yeah, he's not my type." I thought he was beautiful on the inside. Not so much the outside.

"Hey." Brian approached the table with a drink in hand, standing beside Kat. He was handsome as ever, fit in that t-shirt. He had a nice smile, perfectly straight and white teeth.

But instead of being excited, I felt a tightness in my stomach, a drop of dread. "Hey…"

"What's going on, Kat?" he asked.

"We were just talking about this guy I'm seeing." She was normal, not thinking this interaction was weird at all.

"Good things?" he asked.

"He's really hot," she said.

"Good. That's really the only requirement that matters."

Brian always got along with my friends, so he was nice to keep around. We could be alone together or go out to the bar or bowling with my crew. But all that disappeared overnight when Dax came into my life. I never called it off because there was never a right time. I wondered if I should do it now.

Brian looked at me next. "Black is definitely your color."

I was in a black dress and heels, my hair pulled back slightly to show my earrings. "Thanks."

Kat glanced back and forth between us before she guided him closer to me then took his previous spot, so we wouldn't have to talk across her.

Brian's hand immediately went around my waist, and he pulled me close.

But it didn't feel right. It felt like I was doing something I shouldn't. I grabbed his hand immediately and pulled it away. "Brian, I want to talk."

"Oh no. That's not good." He gave me a smile, but his heart wasn't in it.

"I don't think we should see each other anymore."

"Were we ever really seeing each other?" he asked. "I thought I was just your boy toy?"

"Yes, but I'm seeing someone now, and I think it might get serious."

Disappointment flooded his gaze. "I thought you weren't interested in monogamy?"

"I wasn't, but then I met someone... I don't know." I noticed Kat making weird faces behind him, so I shifted my gaze to her.

She kept nodding past me, her eyes open and wide.

I raised an eyebrow.

Then she pointed and started making a stabbing motion.

Brian noticed my distraction and glanced over his shoulder to look at her.

She quickly grabbed her glass and took a big gulp, acting like nothing happened.

Brian turned back to me. "Baby, come on. We're great together."

"I know, but it doesn't feel right anymore." Now that Dax had confronted me about my heartbreak, I realized how much hurt I'd been carrying, how I did everything possible to ignore the pain—instead of moving on. It was time to be vulnerable, to take a chance, to hope for something better and meaningful. So, this didn't feel right any longer, this casual fling. I really liked Dax, wanted it to grow into something, and doing something stupid could jeopardize that.

He sighed. "Well, this guy must be something."

I shrugged, unsure what to say.

"Call me if it doesn't work out. I'm happy to be your rebound." His arm moved around my waist, and he pulled me in for a hug.

Kat started to point again, indicating somewhere behind me.

I cocked an eyebrow and raised one hand in confusion while Brian hugged me.

She tried to mouth something.

Brian pulled away, gave me a smile, and then returned to his crew on the other side of the bar.

I stared at Kat. "Okay, what was all that about?"

"I think she was trying to warn you about me." His deep voice revealed his identity, and he was close behind me at the table.

Kat downed her glass until it was empty and carried it to the bar to get another.

My heart sank into my stomach, and I lost all my confidence. Had he been standing there the entire time? I slowly turned around until I faced him, seeing him in a dark gray V neck that showed the tops of his pecs in the cut of the fabric. He had a scotch on the table, and he looked at me with that smoldering stare that was sexy and terrifying. I didn't know how much he'd heard, how he would feel about what happened, if the fact that I dumped someone to be exclusive with him would just make him uncomfortable. So, for the first time in my life, I was speechless.

He came closer to me, his thick arm circling my waist, hugging the arch in my back. His lips came closer to mine, forcing my pulse to quicken in my neck. "Sweetheart, you're so obsessed with me."

My eyes rolled gently at the taunt.

"You were all over me last night, and now this? You've got it bad. Really bad."

I started to feel embarrassed, knowing all my cards were on the table and he could see them. "Shut up, Dax."

"You shot that guy down because you're sprung on me... pretty sexy."

I rolled my eyes again. "I just didn't—"

He cupped my face and kissed me, his fingers moving deep into my hair, his kiss scorching, wet, and full of heated breath.

I lost my train of thought.

When he pulled away, he was serious, his eyes focused. His hands slowly slid out of my hair as he stared me down. "I don't want to see anybody else either. I haven't been with anyone since I met you...because you're the only woman I want."

I swallowed the lump in my throat, my pulse quickening for a whole new reason. "Looks like you're the one who's obsessed..."

A soft smile entered his lips at my words, his eyes showing the same kind of affection. "Damn right. And I'm not ashamed to say it."

TWENTY

CARSON

Charlie leaned against my desk in my cubicle, his arms crossed over his chest. "And he was just standing there?"

"Kat tried to warn me, but I had *no* idea what she was saying."

"You still didn't think to turn around?"

"She was making these stabbing motions with her finger. I thought she hated Brian or something."

He chuckled. "Then what happened?"

"Dax teased me for being sprung on him—"

"Which you are."

I gave him a playful kick. "And he said he didn't want to see anybody else either."

"What did I tell you?" The cubicles nearby were vacant because people were out of the office, doing their research with their sources. "I told you he was a good guy. Now you're in a relationship, which is great."

"I don't think this constitutes a relationship."

"If you're monogamous with someone, that's a relationship."

"Or an exclusive fling," I countered.

"But it's not a fling. Just accept it, Carson. This is a relationship. And he's a great guy."

"Well...there's still that weird vibe from him." I didn't think Dax was shady, but I definitely thought he was hiding something from me. If it was something personal and none of my business, that was fine. But I worried it was something worse than that.

He shook his head. "I'm sure it's fine."

"What if he's still married or something—"

"He's not." He rolled his eyes. "I know he seems too good to be true, but he's not. He's real. He gets along with your friends, puts up with your bullshit, isn't some misogynistic asshole. He's the right man for you."

I sighed and looked away. "Maybe you should date him—you love him so much."

"If I were gay, I totally would."

I chuckled and stared at my computer screen. "Now get out of here. I've got shit to do."

"Hold on. How are things going with Kat and Nathan?"

I felt like the narrator in this Shakespearean play. "They're hitting it off. Why?"

He tightened his arm across his chest and stared at me for a long time. "I saw Denise the other day... Sometimes I wonder if she knows how I feel about her."

"Well, you make it pretty obvious, dumbass."

He smiled slightly. "And if she does know and doesn't act weird, like try to avoid me, it makes me think she'd be open to the idea." He stared at me, as if expecting some kind of feedback.

"She's never commented on you."

"Not once?"

I shrugged. "Maybe because you're my roommate?"

"Why don't you ask her?"

"Oh my god, I'm not asking her if she thinks you're hot."

"Come on, why not?"

"Because I would be actively pushing you and Denise together, and that feels like a betrayal to Kat."

He sighed.

"You do realize I'm literally in the middle of all three of you?"

He bowed his head.

"If Kat ever knew I had a hand in pushing you together, she would be so hurt, Charlie. If you want something to happen with Denise, then you need to talk to her yourself."

"But I don't want to hurt Kat."

"I understand that...and she's not ready." I wouldn't throw her under the bus and tell Charlie all the things she told me, but I didn't pretend that she was totally over the breakup either.

He didn't react to that. "I hope Nathan erases me."

"You guys were together for two years, Charlie. It's pretty reasonable that she's taking her time."

"I understand," he said quietly. "Honestly, I wish I'd never met Denise. Kat and I were pretty happy together."

That made two of us. I hated mutual friends dating because when they broke up, it made everything complicated. If Charlie dated Denise, it would make things weird with Kat, and if Charlie and Denise broke up, it would make things weird with everyone except Matt.

"When are you going to see Dax again?"

"Not sure—" Just then, my phone lit up on the desk with a message from him.

"Wow," Charlie said. "Not your boy toy anymore, huh?"

I grabbed the phone, suppressing a smile. "He saw it one night and asked me to change it."

He pushed off the desk and started to walk away. "I like where this is going, Carson. Keep it up."

I looked at his message when Charlie was gone. *Dinner tonight?*

Sure.

Wear something nice.

I liked that he took me out to nice places, but I didn't want him to spend his change on me when I was perfectly happy getting a hot dog from a cart on the street. It didn't seem like he had much money, and I didn't want him to blow through his funds on me. *How about I wear lingerie, and we eat a pizza at your place?*

Wear your lingerie under your dress. You can show me after dinner.

I really didn't want him to spend his money on a meal, so I would just pay for it, then. I probably had a higher salary than he did, and if he knew that, it didn't seem like he cared, which was really sexy. He wasn't intimidated by other people's success because he was so secure. In jeans and a t-shirt, he looked like a million bucks. He was a million bucks without having a single bill in his wallet. *Tell me where to meet you.*

THE RESTAURANT WAS an upscale place on the Upper East Side.

The Upper East Side.

I stopped outside the restaurant and realized it was fancy-pants, Michelin-star type of shit.

Why were we eating here?

I didn't mind paying for dinner, but I didn't want to drop two hundred dollars on food that wouldn't keep me full very long. I'd probably hit up a taco shop on the way home because my stomach would growl on the walk.

I stepped inside and found him standing near a table, talking to a guy dressed in slacks and a collared shirt, with a woman in a dress at his side. They all laughed at something Dax said, and then he shook hands with the guy before he kissed the woman on the cheek. They walked away.

I approached the table.

He turned to me, his hands in his pockets, and looked me up and down appreciatively. He was in a gray collared shirt with black slacks, his jaw clean of hair, his eyes sexy and dark. "Damn." He raised his finger and twirled it slightly. "Give me a turn."

"Come on." I rolled my eyes and felt my cheeks blush.

"Sweetheart, I want to get a good look at you." He didn't seem to care about the crowded restaurant, if anyone was staring at us. "It's backless, isn't it? Tell me it's backless."

I set down my clutch and gave a single turn.

"Yes."

I faced him again, feeling hot and bothered by his attention. His compliments were truly flattering since he could have any woman he wanted, but he chose to spend his time with me.

He smiled slightly as he moved into me, his arm circling my waist as he lowered his lips to kiss me. His hand slid down slightly and gave my ass a gentle squeeze.

I didn't push it away because I liked it. I liked having that big hand on my ass, liked the way he claimed me in front of an entire room full of people.

When he turned away, he pulled out the chair for me.

I sat down and let him push me in.

When he sat down across from me, he grabbed the bottle of wine he'd already ordered and filled our glasses. "I made sure they brought the bread right away."

"Wow, someone's trying to get laid." I dug my hand into the basket and grabbed a piece.

"With you, always." He opened his menu and looked at the selections.

I took the opportunity to stare at him, to see the strong cut of his jawline, his simple nose, and his focused eyes. His shoulders were so broad that he could balance a plate on each one.

"What are you thinking, sweetheart?"

I grabbed the menu and almost threw up at the prices. Fifty dollars for a salad? Was the salad shipped from Italy on a private plane? And twenty bucks for soup? Was this shit sprinkled with gold? "Soup."

"And?"

"And that's it."

He cocked an eyebrow as he continued to stare at his menu. "The portions are small here, so I suggest you get something else."

"I'm good."

He put the menu down. "I'm gonna try the sea bass. I hear good things about it."

"Where?"

"At work."

I ripped the bread into pieces and placed each one in my mouth.

He drank his wine as he stared at me. "What is it?"

"What is what?"

"Your mood just plummeted. Why?"

I was never one to sugarcoat anything. I was candid about my thoughts, which made me both popular and unpopular. "I just don't understand why we need to go somewhere so expensive. I'm pretty laid-back. A couple tacos and some beer is a great evening if you ask me."

He rested his arms on the table and stared at me for a while. "Just wanted to take you somewhere nice."

"Well, I like you for you, not because of where you take me. So…this is really unnecessary."

He stared at me for a long time, his hand on his wineglass, his body still. Seconds passed, growing longer until an entire minute disappeared. His expression was stoic, his thoughts a mystery, but something about what I said registered to him. "I appreciate your saying that."

Something about his tone made me rigid. He seemed to say more without really saying anything at all. "How about we ditch this place and get some tacos?"

"No. Let's enjoy ourselves."

"Then we're splitting the bill—"

"Sweetheart, let's not do this." He grabbed his glass and took a drink. "I invited you to dinner because I wanted to take you out. Don't worry about the bill. Let's just have a good time."

"But it's expensive—"

"Don't worry about it."

"You don't seem like Mr. Moneybags, and I don't want you to waste your cash."

He swirled his wine as he regarded me. "Is that a problem?"

"What?"

"That I'm not Mr. Moneybags?"

"Of course not." I didn't understand the question. "It just doesn't make sense to spend your cash impressing a woman who's going to ride your dick at the end of the night regardless if we get a pizza or a gourmet meal. The outcome is the same. May as well save some money."

He smiled slightly. "Ride my dick, huh?"

"Like a cowgirl."

He took another drink of his wine. "Don't torture me, sweetheart." He set his glass down then fished out a slice of bread.

"So, who were you talking to when I walked inside?" I dropped the money issue because it didn't seem to matter at this point, and I didn't want to make our entire evening about finances.

"A colleague."

"A lot of you guys eat here?" I asked in surprise.

"We have company dinners here sometimes. Our Christmas party is held here annually."

"Wow...that's nice." We did a Secret Santa exchange for items that cost less than ten bucks at the paper.

"Yeah. The food is great. So, what are you getting besides that soup?"

I grabbed the menu again.

"And if you don't order something else, I'll order for you."

"Bossy, huh?"

"Oh, you have no idea." He drank his wine as he looked at me.

I held his gaze for a moment before I turned to the menu. "The chicken looks good."

"I've had it. I recommend it."

When the waitress came by, we handed over our menus and gave our orders.

When she was gone, I spoke. "Do you bring other dates here?"

He didn't grow flustered by the question. "No."

"Really?" I asked in surprise.

"I haven't gotten this far with a woman since my divorce. I've been playing the field, just seeing what's out there. And there's not much, by the way."

"New York is full of gorgeous women. What are you talking about?"

"A woman can be drop-dead gorgeous, but that doesn't mean she's a good person."

It was the first time I'd met a guy who didn't prioritize looks.

"I mean, for the night, that's fine. But anything more than that is pretty much unbearable when you despise the person."

"I didn't realize you were actively looking for a relationship." I thought he was just getting over his marriage, just having fun, getting back in the game.

"I wasn't." He held my gaze, not blinking, totally confident. "But then I heard you tell off that guy, and I was hooked."

I smiled. "I thought I was the one hooked on you?"

"Yeah, but I was first." He had a subtle smile on his lips, a playfulness in his eyes. "And I'm not ashamed to say that."

This guy really did seem too good to be true. He was vulnerable with me, honest, and so good-looking it hurt sometimes. I didn't think I could fall for a guy again, but I was starting to sink into the ground. The paranoid side of me thought this was all just some act to get me to sleep with him, but he already had slept with me without all the lies. So, I decided to stop thinking that way, to believe in what he told me. "I know we haven't really talked about what this is, but I stopped seeing Brian because I just didn't want to anymore."

With his hands on the table, he watched me, studying every expression I made.

"And I want you, so I'm willing to get out of my comfort zone. I'm willing to grow and try. But I'm honestly not ready for anything serious. I'm happy to be exclusive and spend time with you, but I just...need to go at my own pace."

He gave a slight nod.

"I'm hopeful that it can be serious someday, just not today."

"Sweetheart, I'm in no rush either. Let's just see where it goes."

"Alright." I grabbed my glass of wine.

"I'm in a good place in my life right now, but I have trust issues. I've still got a lot of baggage from my marriage, so I'm not eager to rush into something new. But when I met you, I knew I needed to make sure you didn't slip away. Another woman like you wasn't going to come along again. So, it sounds like this is perfect for both of us, taking it slow... moving on...but together."

HIS BACK WAS to the couch, his hands on my ass cheeks, kneading them with his large fingers, guiding me up and down at the pace he liked, my cream smearing across the latex condom that kept his flesh apart from mine. Even though I was the one doing all the work, his chest gleamed with sweat, like watching me ride him like a cowgirl was exerting. His pecs were hard and flexed, and the cords in his neck bulged. Sometimes his eyes were on my tits, watching them move up and down, and sometimes they were on my belly, looking at my piercing. And other times, he looked at my face, his eyes getting lost in mine.

Man, he was hot.

His fingers dug into my ass and played with my cheeks, spreading them apart, squeezing them. He would occasionally moan, especially when I lowered myself onto his lap and took the whole thing without wincing. He was a big man with a dick that could demolish a small woman, but every ounce of pain was worth all the pleasure.

Why would his wife ever cheat on him? What a psycho.

His thumb moved to my clit, and he rubbed it harshly, circling round and round and getting my hips to buck slightly in response. I'd already come once, and he was probably eager for me to come again so he could finish. He was a man of restraint, never blowing his load too soon and leaving me hanging.

What a gentleman.

My nails dug into his chest, and I rocked up and down, finishing myself off, making me release a long moan, as if I didn't just find relief minutes ago. My nails dragged through his flesh and sweat, and I slowed my pace, so satisfied I almost forgot about him.

His arms wrapped around my waist, and he tugged me closer to his body, getting my hips to roll as I took his length. He showed me how he wanted to come, the pace he wanted my pussy to move over his dick. He released a loud breath, like the stress was gone from his body because he didn't have to fight his urges anymore. "Ride that dick, sweetheart."

My arms circled around his neck, and I brought my lips to his to kiss him as I rolled my hips, taking that big dick over and over, feeling it thicken inside me as he prepared to release. He was aroused by my kisses the way I was aroused by his.

He moaned into my mouth as he started to come, as his cock twitched inside me and released. He closed his eyes and stopped kissing me, swept up in the desire taking him away.

His fingers dug deep into my flesh, and he bucked against me uncontrollably, shoving his cock deeper and harder. Then he stilled, filling the condom with a satisfying ending.

It was my job to make him feel as good as he made me feel.

Successfully completed.

He relaxed into the couch, looking at me with lazy lidded eyes. He glanced over my body once more, admiring it appreciatively. "Your figure is unbelievable." He grabbed my tits and gave them a gentle squeeze before his hands moved to my waist.

"It's all those pizzas and sandwiches."

He chuckled. "Goes straight to these tits."

I got off him and walked into the bathroom, which didn't even have a shower curtain for the bathtub. I cleaned off and fixed my hair and passed him on the way back. I snagged my panties from the floor and pulled them on before I sat on the couch again.

He came out a moment later and pulled on his black boxers. He fell into the couch beside me, his hand moving to my thigh. He looked at me, a small smile on his lips, still sleepy.

"I should probably head home..."

"Or you could stay."

"I've got a long day tomorrow."

"I hope we aren't starting that all over again."

"I really do have a long day tomorrow."

"Alright." His smile remained. "I'll walk you home."

"Don't be ridiculous." I got to my feet and grabbed my dress. "I smoke with the mob and shake down corporations. I can walk myself home."

"Not dressed like that." He pulled on his shirt then grabbed his slacks from the floor.

"Oh honey, I could walk home naked and be just fine."

"Yeah, I find that unlikely."

I got dressed and slipped on my heels. "Really, it's fine."

"Really, I'm walking you home. That's final."

"That's final?" I asked, cocking my head slightly. "Did you really just go there?"

"Yeah. I did." He buttoned his pants and secured his belt. His playful attitude was gone, and now he looked serious, staring down at me like he was my boss and I was his assistant or something. He slid his hands into his pockets and stared at me, daring me to defy him.

When my heels were secure, I rose to my feet. "I don't appreciate being bossed around."

"Then we're gonna have a problem because I'm a bit bossy."

"You've never shown that quality until now."

"Because you're getting to know me better." He grabbed my clutch off the table and handed it to me. "Come on."

I rolled my eyes. "You say you admire my fire and the way I stand up to people, but then something as routine as walking home—"

"Not routine. Not when you're in a backless dress like that." He grabbed his things by the door and stepped out. "Either sleep here or let's go. Make a decision."

I was frustrated with his behavior, but I also couldn't stay angry for long, not when he had good intentions. I joined him in the hallway, and after he locked the door, we left the building together.

His arm moved around my waist, and he walked with me up the sidewalk, the summer humidity still potent even long after the sun had set. His warm hand stayed against the bare skin of my back, strong but also soft. "I have an idea."

"Yeah?"

He held me close as he stared straight ahead. "It's just you and me, right?"

I didn't understand the question, so I gave him a perplexed expression.

"We're exclusive," he explained. "So why don't we do what exclusive people do?"

"Have a drawer at each other's places?" I asked incredulously.

"No," he said with a chuckle. "Skip the condoms."

I'd only been with one man that way—and that was because I was married to him. I faced forward again and kept walking. "That's too serious for me."

"If it's just the two of us, shouldn't we enjoy it more?"

I shook my head. "That's just too much for me right now."

He let it go. "Alright, I understand. But I hope it's not because you don't trust me."

"I just...don't want that." It was too intimate, especially for me when I was finally putting myself back together. I said I was willing to try with this man, and that was just recently. This seemed rushed.

"Okay." He kept his hand on my back and didn't withdraw his affection.

When we made it to my building, he walked me to my door, his hair messy from the way I'd fisted it on the couch. It was odd that he put on his dinner attire to walk me home instead of something more casual. Wouldn't he have thrown on a t-shirt and jeans or something? "Well, thanks for walking me."

"Sure." He pulled me close and kissed me goodbye, his hand sliding into my hair. "I'll see you later. Goodnight."

"Goodnight."

Before he walked away, he gripped my ass cheek and gave it a playful squeeze. "Have a good day tomorrow, sweetheart." He walked down the hallway, his broad shoulders powerful, his muscular arms swaying by his sides, his ass tight in his slacks.

It made me forget my annoyance.

I stepped inside the apartment.

Charlie was on the couch with the TV on, reading through paperwork. "How'd it go?" he asked without looking at me.

"We had a good time. God, he's so good at sex." I sat in the armchair.

"Good to know." He finished reading his last sentence before he looked at me. "No wonder he was good, since you're dressed like that."

"I look pretty good, huh?" I winked.

He chuckled. "You've looked worse."

"Wow, what a compliment."

He set his paperwork on the coffee table. "You guys had a good time?"

"Yeah. He took me to another fancy place." I rolled my eyes. "I said I want tacos and beer next time, that the expensive stuff doesn't impress me."

"And what did he say?"

"He was cool with it. But the dinner was like two hundred bucks. I offered to split it, but he wouldn't let me, which was kinda a relief because I didn't want to spend a hundred bucks on a single meal…and I'm still hungry. I mean, that's how much I spend on food in a week, you know?"

He shrugged. "Just trying to be a good guy. Can't fault him for that."

"I know." I grabbed my clutch to pull out my phone. But it wasn't there. "Oh shoot…"

"What?"

"I think I left my phone at his apartment. Give me yours."

He grabbed it from the table and tossed it to me.

I caught it and made the call with the phone to my ear. It rang. "Good thing you're crushing on him and have his number."

He rolled his eyes.

It went to voice mail. "Damn, he's ghosting you."

"He's probably walking and doesn't feel it vibrating in his pocket."

I got to my feet and headed to my bedroom. "I can't walk all the way back in heels, so I'm going to change and head out."

"I'll go with you."

"Don't be ridiculous, Charlie." I went into my bedroom and pulled on jeans and a shirt. When I came back, Charlie was ready to go. "I seriously don't need you to take me."

"It's almost eleven."

"So? You've never done this chivalrous stuff before, so why start now?"

"Because you don't have a phone, dumbass."

"Give me yours."

"So you can call me?" he snapped.

I rolled my eyes and walked out.

Charlie came with me, and we walked to Dax's apartment on the same route. It was only a few blocks away, but it felt like a whole different world by the time we got there.

"Are you sure he's even here?"

"Where else would he go at eleven in the evening?" I approached his door and knocked.

"Then why didn't he call me back?"

"Probably because it's eleven at night. If it were me, he probably would have answered." I stood in front of his door and waited.

No sound.

Charlie waited, staring at me, growing more suspicious by the second. "I don't think he's here..."

"Then where would he go?" I felt the dread in my chest, the anxiety that rattled my nerves. Why would he drop me off and then disappear? The only logical explanation was something terrible, like he still had a wife and he went home to her, that this apartment was just a fuck pad. "He's married, isn't he?"

"Whoa, let's not jump to conclusions—"

"Why don't you see the evidence right in front of you?"

"Maybe he went by the store on the way home or something—"

"Right now?" I asked incredulously. "Charlie, come on. I know you've got the hots for him—"

"He deserves the benefit of the doubt, alright? Why would he be trying so hard with you when he could have just left it alone and got sex on a regular basis? Doesn't make sense." He pulled out his phone and texted Dax. *We're outside your door. Carson forgot her phone inside your apartment.* "I'm sure he'll have a good answer."

I crossed my arms over my chest. "I swear to fucking god, if he's a two-timing piece of shit—"

"Just chill, alright?"

The phone started to ring, and his name popped up.

Charlie answered right away. "Hey, man. Where are you?"

"Hey, Charlie. I had to help out a friend. I'll be there in like five minutes."

"Alright. We'll be here." He hung up.

"Help out a friend?" I crossed my arms over my chest. "It's..." I grabbed his phone so I could see the screen. "11:27."

"Well, it wasn't eleven when his friend called."

"But what could he possibly be doing?"

Charlie looked away.

"Why aren't you more upset about this?"

He shook his head and turned back to me. "Because...I don't want you to be right. Dax seems like a great guy, and if he's not, then he's a pathological liar, and that's just...really depressing. I don't want to live in a world where people are this evil... I can't do it. So, I'd rather keep hoping for the best."

I leaned against the door and sighed, feeling the dread in my chest, the fear gripping me by the throat.

Charlie leaned against the door too. "Let's not jump to conclusions, alright?"

"Sorry, it's my job. I look at evidence and make conclusions."

"But we don't have all the evidence. You're making unfair assumptions."

I rolled my eyes.

Dax walked down the hallway minutes later, in the clothes he'd dropped me off in. He was smiling at me, retaining his calm and cool composure. "Hey." He pulled his keys out of his pocket as he approached the door. "Sweetheart, you don't have to leave your phone behind just to see me again." He got it unlocked then stepped inside.

Charming asshole.

"I could have brought it to you." He picked it up from the floor where it had fallen off the table.

"It's fine. Charlie didn't mind coming with me." I took the phone and slipped it into my pocket. "I would have waited until tomorrow, but I need it for work."

"I understand." His arm circled my waist, and he gave me a kiss. "No explanation needed."

I kissed him back, but my heart wasn't totally in it. "Is your friend okay?"

His eyes narrowed on my face for a second. "Yeah. He asked me to go by the pharmacy and grab something for him. He was discharged from the hospital recently. He broke his leg, so it's hard for him to get around."

"Oh no, sorry to hear that," Charlie said.

"Yeah," I said, wanting to believe him but not entirely convinced he was telling the truth. "Well, we should get going…"

He headed to the door. "Goodnight." He gave me another kiss before I walked out.

"See you later, man." Charlie shook his hand.

"Get my girl home safely." He stood in the doorway, one hand on the knob.

I rolled my eyes. "I can get my ass home safely on my own." I turned to walk away.

His voice came from behind me, addressing Charlie. "Damn, isn't she sexy?" He shut the door.

Charlie caught up with me. "He seemed normal to me."

"Yeah..."

"If he's hiding anything, he's a criminal mastermind. And I just don't believe that."

It was hard for me to believe too, but something still felt off.

"Don't worry about it."

"Alright." I tried to push it from my mind, to not be a person who assumed everyone was a liar any time a story didn't quite fit. I really liked Dax, more than I should, and he was such a positive thing in my life that I didn't want to jeopardize it...even if it meant my heart was at risk.

TWENTY-ONE
DAX

I sat in my chair near the window, leaning back with my elbow on the armrest, my eyes on the view of the city, the other skyscrapers and the glimpse of Central Park as it extended for miles. I'd been sitting there for a while, various thoughts going through my mind, both business and personal.

A knock sounded on my office door.

Very few people just came to my door, so I knew who it was. "Come in." I turned in my chair, facing my desk and the rest of my office, the two couches and the coffee table, the large double doors that led to my two assistants who faced each other at their desks.

My sister stepped inside, carrying a folder of paperwork. She was in a navy-blue dress with a black jacket on top, her long hair pulled over one shoulder. Her heels tapped against the floor as she approached my desk. "Bad day?"

My only response was my stare.

"I'll take that as a yes." She set the folder on my desk. "Everything is in there."

I pulled it close to me, opened it, and flipped through the numbers.

She took a seat and looked outside, admiring the sunshine that illuminated the city.

I took my time reading through it, licking my fingers and thumbing through each page.

"Ugh, I hate it when you do that."

I glanced at her, licked my thumb, and dragged it down the center of the page.

"Real mature."

I returned everything to the folder and tossed it back onto the desk. "It's fine."

"You can keep them." She held up her hand, not interested in the paperwork that was full of my licks. "I'll just print another copy."

I propped my cheek against my knuckles, staring at her, both annoyed and relaxed in her presence.

She stared at me for a while. "She didn't take the deal."

"I know."

"How?"

"Because if she had, that would have been the first thing out of your mouth."

Slowly, a look of pity came over her face. "She's purposely useless so she doesn't have to work, and she continues to collect her paycheck like she's employee of the month." She didn't directly accuse me of anything, but the resentment was there, deep under the skin, hidden in her gaze.

"I'm sorry, Renee."

"I don't blame you—"

"Yes, you do."

She sighed quietly, her shoulders lifting with the breath she took.

"And you have every right to." I hadn't taken my father's advice when I'd married her. I was an arrogant dumbass who risked the company that had been in my family for two generations. I gave my marriage everything, not realizing I was giving my family nothing. I shouldn't be sitting in this chair at this point. Didn't fucking deserve it.

"We'll figure something out…eventually."

I didn't have any options. I'd tried to buy her out many times, but there was never any price high enough—not when she could get a fat check every month for the rest of her life. "What's new with you?" I didn't want to talk about her anymore. I didn't want to spend any of my precious time thinking of my gravest mistake.

"William and I went to dinner last night."

"Sounds like it's getting serious."

She shrugged. "Might be." Renee was beautiful, looking so much like my mother, it seemed as if she were still here even though she'd been sleeping in her grave for years. She was also smart, talented, and funny…so she could have any guy she wanted. But there never seemed to be a serious man in her life.

Maybe my horrific marriage scared the fucking shit out of her.

It would scare anyone. "Should I meet this guy?"

She released a quiet laugh. "So you can run him off?"

"I wouldn't do that."

She turned back to me, one eyebrow raised.

"I wouldn't," I repeated.

"Uh-huh…"

"If I liked him, I wouldn't."

"And I doubt you'll ever like anyone."

"You're the pickiest woman I know, so I trust your quality-assurance program."

She rolled her eyes, but there was a smile on her lips. "Let me think about it."

"First of all, do *you* like him? Because that's the most important thing here."

"Yes."

"Like, really like him?"

"I don't usually let myself like anyone until they pass all the tests."

"Has he?"

She nodded.

I started to count on my fingers. "Honest?"

She nodded.

"Kind?" I held up a second finger.

"Yep."

"Got a job?"

She rolled her eyes. "You think I'm gonna date a guy without a job?"

"Just going through the motions here. Does he like sports?"

"Why does that matter?"

"Want to make sure we have something in common."

"So, you have to have something in common with my boyfriend to like him?"

"It would certainly help. Does he play basketball?"

"Uh, I'm not sure."

"Golf?"

"I'm pretty sure he golfs."

"Good."

She shook her head slightly. "Now I want you to meet him even less."

"Well, I'm gonna meet the guy eventually, so there's no avoiding it."

"But you can try to be cool about it."

"Mom and Dad aren't around anymore, so it's my job not to be cool about it."

She thought I was joking and got to her feet. "I have to get back to my desk. See you later."

I didn't want to give the guy a hard time, but I didn't want my sister to make the same mistakes I did. I didn't want her to be not only heartbroken, but humiliated, ashamed. I carried that every single day, and it was worse when I had to look my ex in the eye—the eyes of the fucking devil.

AFTER WORK, I met Clint at the bar. I was in my suit, as was he.

He sat at the table alone, tucked in the corner because it was the table always given to him when he came in to spend money. He was already drinking when I walked in. "You look like shit. Did you see that cunt today?"

"Not in the flesh." All I did was raise my hand, and the waitress brought my regular drink—a scotch, neat. I grabbed the glass and took a drink, wiping my lip with my thumb when a drop missed my mouth. "But I can feel her presence in the building—because it's five thousand degrees."

He chuckled. "Her horns poke through the ceiling, too?"

"Wouldn't be surprised. What's up with you?"

He shrugged. "Made some money. Lost some money. You know how it goes."

"No. I tend not to lose money."

"You lost quite a bit when your divorce went public."

I gave him a cold glare.

"Alright, that was low."

I drank from my scotch.

"So, how's it going with that sassy reporter?"

I sighed as I looked into my glass then dragged my hand down my face, feeling the guilt, the anger, all the self-loathing.

"Damn...sorry I asked."

"Everything with her is fine." I straightened and dropped my hand to the table. "I'm really into her."

"Then what's with the bad mood?"

"Because..." I stared into my scotch, seeing the dark liquid staring back at me. "I keep lying to her."

"Come on, you have to protect yourself. The second a woman knows who you are, it changes everything. It's not fair to you."

"I know. But she was at my fake apartment last night and left her phone behind. When she went back to get it, I wasn't there. I had to tell my driver to turn around and haul ass to get back there. Then I lied about helping a friend...at eleven at night."

"But you would help a friend at that time of night."

"That's not the point. I'm not sure if she was suspicious or not, but it just felt...dirty."

"Then tell her."

I didn't want to do that either. Since I actually liked her, I was afraid it would change everything.

"How upset can she really be?" he asked incredulously. "When she finds out you're a billionaire, she'll probably be excited. She won't have to sleep in a shitty apartment. She'll come to your penthouse and check out that view. Party with us on the yacht. You know, live life in the fast lane. Trust me, she's not going to give a damn that you lied."

I really didn't know how she would feel about it. She didn't seem like a woman who cared about wealth. She was annoyed every time we went to a fancy place, and she always attested tacos were just fine. When we came back to my apartment, she never teased me for how barren it was. She came back time and time again. So, would my wealth change anything? Or would the lie be the reason she lost her temper?

I did feel guilty about that.

"You've got to tell her at some point, right? I mean, if you want to keep seeing her."

"I do want to keep seeing her."

"Then just do it," he said with a shrug. "Hey, are you going to the lingerie party tomorrow night? Brad and Joel are both down."

"Of course they are."

"You coming?"

I'd been doing all the typical billionaire playboy bullshit for the last year, and it felt just as empty as my broken marriage. It was inappropriate to be there when I had an exclusive relationship with someone, even if she wasn't my girlfriend or something more. "No."

"What? You're joking."

"No."

"It's sexy women in panties…"

"I understand that, Clint," I said sarcastically. "I just googled the word lingerie."

"And you aren't going to go?"

"I'm seeing Carson."

"You don't have to fuck anybody. You can at least look."

I'd rather see Carson in lingerie. I still had her pictures on my phone. "You'll have fun without me."

"There's no doubt of that. I just feel bad for you."

"Don't."

He drank from his glass. "What's so interesting about this reporter? Reporters are the worst, man."

"They're only the worst when you have something to hide."

"Well, I do have things to hide."

"Oh, I know."

"But for real?" he asked. "I'm sure she's beautiful, but aren't they all?"

There were beautiful women everywhere, but beauty was the least important thing to me now. Beauty wasn't synonymous with good. I'd been seduced by my ex-wife, who was gorgeous, but it was all a ploy—and I fell for it. It was a hard lesson to learn, but it opened my eyes to the world, showed me that there were more important attributes than looks, such as heart, integrity, and honesty. When I heard Carson telling off that guy in the booth, I listened to every single word, grew more enamored of this woman with a spine harder than mine, than most suits I knew. I was attracted to her strength, her integrity, her ambition—without even seeing her face. I was sitting in a different booth, so I only heard her voice.

But that was enough for me.

I'd gotten up to see what she was drinking, and when I saw her long brown hair, those bright green eyes, those gorgeous legs from underneath her dress...I knew I'd hit the jackpot. I knew there wasn't another woman like her, and despite my baggage, I had to make something happen. The woman I was originally meeting was a fuck buddy, and I knew Carson didn't have the right qualities to be another notch in my bedpost. She was more than that, and I knew it before I even spoke to her.

But I went for it anyway.

I TOOK off my shirt and left it on the bleachers before I joined the guys on the court. They passed me the ball, and I dribbled toward the hoop and made my shot.

All net.

We ran back and forth, working up a sweat, taking our warm-up as seriously as a real game. Sweat dripped down my forehead and chest and made my skin shine under the lights. When Charlie, Matt, and Carson walked in, I called time-out and walked over to them.

Charlie had become a friend quickly because he was a good guy. Instead of being jealous or uncomfortable by Carson's close friendship with a handsome guy, I chose to accept it. Being around them showed me how platonic that relationship was, the way she took me to her apartment and was all over me with Charlie just across the hall. I hadn't believed a straight man and woman could just be friends, but they proved me wrong.

Carson was in little gym shorts and a black tank top. Her thick hair was slicked back into a ponytail, and since she got sweaty on the court, she skipped the makeup. But her features were so distinguished that she didn't really need makeup in the first place. Her eyes were bright entirely on their own, her lips a naturally red color. Her complexion was luminous too, like she took good care of her skin even though she didn't seem to get a full eight hours of sleep every night.

She was gorgeous but also one of the boys.

I loved it.

I moved to Charlie first. "Hey, man."

He closed his fist and tapped his knuckles against mine since my hands were so sweaty. "Ready for this?"

"I'm already worn out from the warm-up, so not so much."

I greeted Matt next. He'd hit it off with my friend Jeremy and they were still seeing each other, and from what Jeremy told me, it was a good match.

Finally, I turned to Carson. "Hey, sweetheart."

"Hey." When she first looked at me, she had a slightly guarded look. It wasn't the expression she used to give me, the same one she gave her friends. But it went away, and her eyes moved up and down my body, looking at my hard physique covered in sweat.

I moved closer to her, my hands cupping her waist as I bent my neck down to look at her. Without her heels, she was significantly shorter than me, so our height differences were apparent. But she was still sexy, still perfect that way.

She didn't care if I touched her with sweaty palms since she would work up a sweat heavier than anyone else. She softened noticeably the longer I touched her, the closer we came together. She tilted her head up to look at me, her eyes always fierce, like she could say a smartass comment at any moment.

I loved that sass. It was one of the things that attracted me to her in the first place. I didn't realize what I wanted in a woman until I met her. Someone independent, who could think for herself, who wasn't afraid to call bullshit when she saw it. She could stand up to men twice her size without blinking.

So fucking sexy.

"I'm excited to guard you for the next hour."

She smiled slightly, but her eyes filled with attitude. "I don't need you to protect me, Dax."

"I know you don't." She had thick skin, like rhino hide. But I wanted to keep her safe, regardless. I was protective of her around the guys, not just because she was mine, but because I'd rather die than see her get hurt. "But I want to."

MOST OF THE guys were faster than her as we sprinted across the court. But she made up for it with her agility, because she was better at handling the ball, passing it discreetly, and her deep connection to Charlie made them great teammates. It was almost cheating because their communication was practically telepathic.

I chose to cover her because I kept my distance and didn't treat her as an adversary. I tried to steal the ball and box her in, but I never became aggressive like the other guys, and when I blocked her, I kept the other guys off her if they tried to steal the ball. So two birds with one stone.

At the end of the match, her team won and we lost.

Again.

We left the court and walked over to the benches where our towels and waters were. Most of the guys headed straight to the locker room. Charlie took a seat and dumped the contents of his bottle on his head before he patted himself dry.

Carson dried off with a towel before she drank everything out of her bottle. Her legs were toned and chiseled, like aerobic exercise kept her body lithe and athletic. She had a flat stomach and large breasts, big enough that they almost looked disproportionate.

But they were nice tits.

I'd like to tit-fuck her sometime.

I sat beside Carson and drank my water. "You were good out there."

"I play to win."

"Yeah?" I smiled, loving her bluntness. "What happens when you don't win?"

"Learn from my mistakes and try again."

And I liked her attitude. She didn't take failure as a defeat, but rather as a stepping-stone. She didn't get offended easily, wasn't sensitive at all, and she held her head high, like one of the guys. Her fierce sense of independence came from somewhere, but I wasn't sure where. I hadn't spent much time with her sister, but she seemed very different from Carson, and not just because she was blond.

"Guys, if we don't eat, I'm going to die," Matt said. "Like, literally."

"Literally?" Charlie asked incredulously.

"Yeah," Matt said. "That's what I said."

Charlie shook his head. "You know that's impossible, right?"

"No, it's not," Matt argued. "If you don't eat, you'll die at some point."

"If you don't eat for like three weeks." Charlie drank from his water bottle. "I think you'll make it an hour."

"You guys want pizza or sandwiches?" Matt asked. "Sandwiches are quicker, so I think I want sandwiches."

"I'd eat a possum right now, so I don't care." Carson placed her towel over her shoulder.

"A possum?" I eyed her, amused.

"I'm starving." She turned to me.

"No wonder you don't like fancy places," I teased.

She narrowed her eyes at me and gave me a playful hit on the arm before she stood up. "Let's go. I think Charlie and I deserve a victory meal for kicking everyone's ass." She walked up to him and gave him a high five.

"Yep." Charlie patted his face once more before he followed her.

I walked beside Charlie. "What's new with you?"

"Nothing," he said. "Just working a lot. I've had to pick up a colleague's work because he's on sick leave."

"Is he going to be okay?" I asked.

"Yeah," Charlie said. "He developed a hernia and needed immediate surgery. Shit happens, you know?"

"Yeah."

We left the gym and went to the sandwich shop. I walked behind Carson and Matt while I continued to talk to Charlie, my eyes on her perky ass most of the time. Other men who walked by craned their necks to look at it before they continued forward.

We walked inside, and one by one, we ordered our food.

I wanted to offer to pay for Carson's dinner, but that would turn into an argument.

After she ordered, she stepped aside for me to order.

"I'll get the turkey club with the combo."

"And we're together." Carson pointed between us as she looked at the cashier. She pulled out some cash from a hidden section of her phone.

"Sweetheart, you don't have to do that." I appreciated the gesture, but she worked hard for her salary, and I had a ton of zeros in my bank account. It didn't seem right to accept anything from her. But at the same time, it was nice to be with a woman who didn't expect anything from me, who wasn't in love with my wallet instead of me.

She handed over the money then stuck her tongue out at me. "It's happening. We aren't doing that bullshit thing where the guy pays for everything. This is a two-way street, man." She picked out a bag of chips then walked to the beverage station, filling her cup with ice and a soda before sitting next to Charlie in the booth near the window.

Matt ordered his food then scooted down the line. "She's a pain in the ass, isn't she?"

I grinned. "I don't mind." I grabbed chips and an empty soda cup.

"Really? She's a pain in the ass to me." He grabbed his chips and turned away.

"I know you don't mean that."

"Oh, I do." He filled his soda then walked to the table.

I did the same then glanced at them together. Charlie had just said something to make Carson laugh, and she ripped open her bag of chips and spilled them all over her napkin and the table. But she ate them anyway.

I joined them, sitting beside Matt and across from Carson. We were all tired from the game, our hair still damp with sweat, and our muscles screamed in exhaustion. Carson devoured her bag of chips, picking them off the table and popping them into her mouth.

"Are you going to kiss her after seeing that?" Charlie asked, holding his bag of chips in one hand while his other hand dug inside and fished out a piece.

"What?" she asked, raising an eyebrow before continuing.

"You're literally eating off the table." Matt eyed her.

"You say literally a lot," she fired back.

"It's a good word." Matt grabbed a handful of chips and put them into his mouth. "So, are you?" He turned to me.

"It takes more than a few dirty chips to scare me off." I left my bag on the table and stared at her, my arms resting on the surface. Even when she looked her worst, she looked her best to me. Her fire kept me warm, her intelligence was refreshing, and she was quick with the comebacks. It was the first time I'd been with a woman where she was more than just a lover, but also a close friend. I could tease her, pick on her, have a hobby with her like playing basketball.

She smiled before she grabbed the last chip off the table. "This guy is all man."

Matt continued to stare at me, his eyes turning dreamy. "I know…"

Charlie kicked him under the table. "Don't come on to him."

"What?" Matt asked incredulously. "I'm just agreeing with Carson."

"It's fine," Carson said. "I'm sure tons of women come on to Dax all the time, so he's used to it." She looked at my bag of chips. "Are you going to eat those?"

A smile came onto my lips, and I flicked them closer to her. "Go for it, sweetheart."

"Do a lot of women come on to you?" Matt asked.

I kept looking at Carson, unsure how to answer the question. "No one compared to Carson."

Charlie nodded as he ate his chips. "Ooh…good answer."

Carson opened my bag of chips and started to eat. "He's just being humble. I'm sure supermodels want his nuts all the time," she said playfully without a hint of jealousy, and that was something else that made her cool. She wasn't easily intimidated.

When I asked her to skip the condoms, I was disappointed by her answer, but I also understood she wasn't ready, that she still had her guard up because we'd only known each other for about a month. She hit the brakes every time I hit the gas, but it was good that one of us was controlling the pace so we wouldn't crash.

I didn't respond to her statement because she was right. But they didn't just want me for me, but because I was a powerful suit with a nice penthouse, my name on the front door of my building. I could get pussy with my looks, but I suspected the money was sexier than my appearance.

I should be grateful for my inheritance, but the money felt like a disservice sometimes. It ruined my life, made people treat me differently, gave me respect from strangers that I didn't deserve. It trapped me in a marriage based on a lie, made me love a woman who never loved me, not even on our wedding day.

Our sandwiches were brought to us.

"Thank god," Matt said, unwrapping the sandwich immediately and taking a bite big enough to rival the jaw of a dinosaur. He even tore through the bread with his teeth, ripping off the piece before he chewed.

Carson ate quickly, just not ferociously. Her hand dived into my bag of chips, and she ate those at the same time.

We turned quiet, our mouths full.

Charlie ate with his elbows on the table, hovering over his food.

Matt demolished everything in record time.

I ate with my eyes on Carson, seeing the way she shifted between sandwich and chips, her eyes on her food instead of me. When she noticed my stare, she turned her bag of chips toward me so we could share.

"That's generous…"

She narrowed her eyes playfully and took another bite.

I reached my hand inside and grabbed a chip before I continued eating. We ate in comfortable silence, like I was part of the group. I'd infiltrated their ranks and felt like I belonged there. We didn't talk about money, the next hot club, when we would take a yacht out…nothing like that. Life was simple, really simple.

And it was nice.

TWENTY-TWO

DAX

I sat on the couch in my penthouse, working on my laptop with the TV on, the breathtaking view of the city in front of me, the Manhattan lights bright. I was in my sweatpants and a t-shirt, scrolling through reports and paperwork.

The doorbell rang before the chef stepped inside. "Good evening, Mr. Frawley." He let himself inside and headed to the table.

"Hello, Chef." I kept my eyes on my computer.

He moved to the table and set up my dinner before he quietly excused himself.

I closed my laptop and walked over to the dining table. There was a Cab from 1970 on the table along with a filled glass, and he'd left a plate of fresh fish with sautéed vegetables with a green salad.

I sat down and ate alone.

My penthouse was in the corner of the building, so I had views from almost anywhere in the apartment. I looked outside as I ate, seeing the light from a helicopter in the distance. The double-paned glass made it impossible to hear the sounds of the city outside, and it gave me a false feeling of calm when there were sirens going off everywhere, pedestrians talking loudly, restaurants packed with people.

I drank my wine and felt the emptiness inside me...deep inside.

My phone buzzed with a text message. *Your sister is here to see you. Shall I let her up?*

I texted back the security officer in the lobby. *Yeah.*

She just got into the elevator.

I didn't get up and continued to eat.

The doors opened a minute later straight into the living room. She stood in the center, in jeans and a blouse, wearing heels that gave her extra inches in height. She had a folder under her arm, and she welcomed herself inside. A watch was on her wrist, and her clothes showed her station in life. "Didn't mean to interrupt your meal."

"It's fine. You want some?"

"No. But I'll take a glass of that wine." She set the folder down and helped herself to a glass in the kitchen before she returned. She sat down and filled the glass before she smelled it. "I love French wine." She swirled it and took a sip. "1980?"

"70."

"Close."

"You were off by a decade." I pulled the folder closer to me but didn't open it.

She took a few more sips, savoring the taste. "How's your dinner?"

"Good."

"I had his lamb chops last night. To die for."

I didn't eat lamb.

She studied me, eyes similar to mine. "Everything alright?"

I shrugged as I ate. My sister and I butted heads, disagreed on a lot of things, but she was the only family I had in the world, so she was like a mother to me in some ways, even though we were close in age. I shared things with her because I didn't have anyone else to share them with. She did the same with me, telling me about the men in her life like she would tell our mother.

She held her glass and took a sip. "You're brooding bad."

"I always brood."

"Yeah, but this is worse than usual. Did Clint piss you off?"

"He always pisses me off, but no."

"Then talk to me."

I hadn't told her about Carson. I'd told my playboy friends, but they didn't seem to care or understand. Monogamy was like the plague, especially after my nasty divorce. "I've been seeing this woman..."

"Oh." She nodded slightly. "And that's bad because...?"

It was bad for a lot of reasons. "I like her."

"It's bad that you like her?" she asked for clarification, as if she'd misheard me. "Dax, not every woman in the world is like Rose. There're good people out there, and I think it's great that you're giving someone a chance. This is the first time I've ever heard you mention anyone, so she must be special to you."

"She is." She was a breath of fresh air after being around egotistical, greedy people all day long. The grass was always greener on the other side, but her yard was like an oasis. She wasn't stupid and airheaded. She was smart…really smart. Her intelligence was so sexy to me.

"Then that sounds like great news."

"Well…she doesn't know who I am."

She propped her chin on her hand as she looked at me. "I don't understand what that means."

I looked at the Manhattan lights as I spoke. "Anytime I meet a woman and she knows who I am, she treats me differently. It's not real. I'm tired of that. So, when I met Carson, I lied…"

"About?"

"Everything." I turned back to her. "She thinks I'm just a financial advisor at the company. I have this little apartment I take girls to so they think I'm average and kinda on the poor side."

She shook her head slightly. "Dax…"

"I've met a few girls that way, and it's a completely different experience. And with Carson, it's been really nice."

"So, what was your goal? Were you looking for a relationship?"

"Not necessarily. I just got really tired of all the bullshit. It's the same kind of girls over and over…"

"Well, have you ever tried to date a normal girl as yourself?"

"Yes. They're either obsessed with my wealth or they're uncomfortable by it. This way, I've been able to meet girls who see me as me. Some like me, and some don't. But it's real."

"How is it real if you're lying?" She drank from her glass.

"It just gives me a genuine opportunity to connect with someone. And I really connect with Carson. I don't love her. I'm not ready to have an intense relationship. But…I want to keep seeing her. We're exclusive. But the longer it continues, the more guilty I feel about the whole thing."

"Well, you are lying."

I closed my eyes and sighed. "I'm not married or have a disease or something. Fundamentally, I'm the same person, whether I have a small apartment or a penthouse. That isn't a lie. My bank account is the lie."

"But still, she thinks you're sleeping in that apartment when it's actually a fuck pad."

I rolled my eyes. "That's not what it is."

"She might feel that way."

I really had no idea how she would feel about it. She was smart, so she would probably understand my point of view. She researched people in my world, so she probably understood the lifestyles of the wealthy. She'd probably understand why I wanted to hide it until I got to know her better.

"If you like her, come clean. Tell her the truth and explain why you lied. If she finds out some other way..." She shook her head. "She might feel used, you know?"

I nodded.

"What kind of field is she in?"

"She's an investigative journalist for the *New York Press*."

Her eyes widened in surprise. "Wow. So, she's a smart cookie."

"Very smart."

"And she hasn't figured out you're a big, fat liar yet?"

Sometimes it seemed like she knew something was off, but she gave me the benefit of the doubt, which made me feel worse. She was actively trying to trust me...and I was lying to her.

Fuck, I was an asshole.

"Dax, talk to her. If you explain yourself, I'm sure she'll understand."

I nodded. "Yeah...I hope so."

"And wow." She drank from her glass then licked her lips. "You're really going after a whole different kind of woman now."

"You haven't met her."

"Just the fact that she has such a serious job is a huge change of pace for you. I mean, Rose is a fucking ditz, and the rest of the women I've seen you with are mindless Barbie dolls."

"Rose isn't a ditz. She wouldn't own a piece of the company if she were."

She sighed in annoyance. "True."

Rose was a manipulative cunt.

"You think I'll meet this woman sometime?"

I shrugged. "We'll see how it goes after I tell her. She may not stick around."

After a final drink, her glass was empty, so she ran her fingers along the edge, smearing her lipstick. "You know, I don't say this much, so don't get used to it. But you're quite the catch, Dax. You're good-looking, kind, understanding, funny. I mean, you probably shouldn't have lied, but she'd be lucky to have you."

I smiled, looking at my sister.

"What?"

"It's just nice to get a compliment from you."

"It's not a regular thing. Don't get used to it." She looked away. "How long have you been seeing her?"

"I met her about a month ago."

Her eyes widened. "Dax...that's a long time."

"I know."

"You need to tell her—sooner rather than later."

TWENTY-THREE
CARSON

The club was heaving with activity. Loud music over the speakers, girls dancing on the floor, men in the booths with their knees obnoxiously far apart. I sat at the bar and finished my margarita as I stared at my target, both of his arms around a woman in a short dress. With greasy black hair and a large nose, he spoke to his crew, a flashy watch on one wrist.

I'd done this a million times, so I wasn't scared.

I finished my drink then marched over there, in a short dress and heels, blending in instead of making it obvious I was a journalist out for blood. I arrived at the area and sat on the circular table facing Omar. I crossed my legs and flipped my hair.

At first, he smiled, like I was another notch on his belt, but then he looked past the big hair and red lips and recognized me. "Bitch is back." His arms slacked on the girls, and he gave me a ferocious scowl.

"Honey, I never left." I flipped my hair again to be obnoxious. "I'm always right behind you. So, you want to talk here or in private?"

"Write about me again, and I'll kill you."

"Uh-huh." I nodded. "You said that before, and yet, I'm still here." I cocked my head and continued to stare. "So how about you just give me what I want, and I'll—"

"Get her out of my face." He waved to his men.

One man moved to my left, but before he could stop me, I pulled out the little knife tucked between my breasts and pointed it right at his balls, which were level with my head. "Touch me, and you'll have bloody balls."

The guy didn't lay a hand on me.

"How did you get that in here?" Omar asked.

I shrugged. "Probably the same way you got that gun in here." I knew he was armed even if I couldn't see it. I jabbed the knife at the guy so he would back off. "Now, let's be civil here. All I want is information."

"Information is everything."

"Couldn't agree more. So, you want to do this here or in private?"

"Sure." He dropped his arms from his girls. "In private."

I tucked the knife down my top again and rose to my feet. I walked ahead, heading out the main doors and past the line of people trying to get in. I stopped on the sidewalk and crossed my arms over my chest.

He kept walking. "You wanted to talk? Let's talk." He stepped into the alleyway.

I was brave but not stupid. I pulled out my knife and hid it in my palm. I joined him in the alleyway, away from the line of people that could see us. "I know you're shipping everything through the barges at the port—"

His hand lashed out and aimed for my throat.

My knife was quick, slashing him down the arm as I kicked him. "Omar, you're better than this."

He turned around, gripping his bloody arm.

I held the knife in my hand, the tip dripping with his blood. "Look, all I want to do is talk. Not reenact Mortal Kombat. But I'll finish you if I have to." I deepened my voice like the narrator in the video game. "Finish him!"

"You fucking bitch." He lunged at me, grabbing my wrist with the knife and throwing it down.

I kicked him right in between the legs. "Honey, you don't know who you're dealing with."

He bowed down to grip his balls but then grabbed me by the neck and prepared to shove me into the wall.

"Fuck off, asshole." A man grabbed him and threw him hard to the ground.

Omar slammed into the asphalt and groaned in pain.

I stared at his back, seeing the man who was over six feet and in a black suit. He looked familiar, with that dark hair and webs of veins on the tops of his hands.

Omar got to his feet, clutching his bloody arm.

The man turned with his movements, keeping his body in between us, acting as a shield as Omar left the alley and turned back to the club.

"I appreciate what you did, but I had it under control—"

"Under control?" He turned around and faced me, with brown eyes, a stern jaw, and that shadow along his chin and part of his cheeks.

My eyes widened. "Dax? What are you doing here?"

He ignored my question. "You could have gotten yourself killed. What the hell are you thinking?"

"I'm doing my job." I flicked the knife down so the blood droplets would leave the blade. Then I tucked it back into the sheath at the front of my dress. "Sometimes, things don't go according to the plan, but I'm prepared."

His hands moved to his hips, and he stepped closer to me, his eyes shifting back and forth in a rageful stare, like he didn't know how to process what just happened. "Getting killed is not part of your job."

"But getting information is, and people don't always want to talk."

"Then you leave it alone," he barked. "An article is not worth getting killed over."

"I disagree." I crossed my arms over my chest.

Now he stared at me incredulously.

"I knew what I signed up for when I took this job. I don't need a lecture."

"I think you do." He raised his voice, growing louder with every passing second. "What if he had a gun?"

"He did, but he didn't use it. See? I know shit."

He gripped his skull and released an angry sigh before he forced himself to calm down. "What if I hadn't been here?"

"You're being dramatic. There are people like fifteen feet away. I could have screamed, and they would have run over here. I promise you, I had it handled."

"He was about to choke you."

"And I was about to stab him right between the ribs. Seriously, I had it covered."

He sighed and dropped his shoulders, clearly irritated with me. "You're alright?"

"Not a scratch." I moved closer to him, dropping my arms to embrace him. My hands moved under his jacket and around his waist, and I leaned in close to kiss him.

His kiss wasn't affectionate right away, a little cold. But once my mouth massaged warmth into his, he got into it, slipped his fingers into my hair, and deepened the kiss.

"I've never seen you in a suit." My hands moved up his chest, playing with his tie. "Sexy."

He smiled slightly at the compliment, his eyes on my lips and then the rest of my body. "Red is your color."

I nodded to the dumpster farther down. "You wanna?" I played with his tie, my eyes on his sexy mouth, wanting to get frisky now that the adrenaline had passed.

"I don't have a condom."

"What?" I stuck my hands into his pockets to check. "Why?"

"Why would I bring condoms to a club if the woman I'm sleeping with isn't there?"

"Hmm...good point." My fingers stroked his tie.

He stared down into my face, watching me touch him.

"I mean...I guess we could skip it." I lifted my gaze and looked at him again, wanting him now that he was in my grasp, seduced by that kiss, the way he intervened even though I didn't need help. The whole thing was sexy, and damn, his shoulders were nice in that suit.

He stared at me for a while, his arms around my waist while his hand squeezed my ass. He pulled me closer and hugged me a little bit, like that was what he wanted more than anything. But his words contradicted that. "Let's go back to your place."

"Really?" I asked. "Did you just turn down sex?"

"No. We're having sex. Just not in an alleyway." He grabbed my hand and walked with me out of the alleyway and to the sidewalk. "And with a condom, because that's what you said you wanted before you were high on adrenaline and whatever else you're on right now." He walked past the club and the line of people and kept walking.

"So, what were you doing here? Why are you in a suit?"

He stared straight ahead for a long time, as if he didn't hear a word I said.

"Dax?"

"I went out with some colleagues."

"So, you wear a suit to work?" Because one time, he went to work in jeans.

"Sometimes." His mood was noticeably down, like he was angry all over again.

"Why are you—"

"When you shake down your sources like that, do you ever get anything accomplished?"

"Sometimes."

"Have you ever gotten hurt?"

"I mean, a black eye here and there but nothing serious."

"Does Charlie go through this?"

"No. He does different kinds of articles, more low-key."

"By choice?" he asked.

"No. He wants to work up to a higher position, but it takes time." Charlie and I were friends but also colleagues. Whenever I moved up higher than him, he never seemed upset about it. He was always happy for me and never behaved otherwise. By nature, he wasn't a competitive person.

"Does it bother him that you got promoted before he did?"

"No. He never says so, at least."

"That's pretty big of him."

"Yeah, he's a great guy."

We walked a few blocks and then entered my building. We reached the apartment and stepped inside.

Charlie was on the couch, eating cereal even though it was nine in the evening. "You were supposed to go to the store today."

"I know. I had to chase down a lead."

Charlie looked me up and down. "Dressed like that?"

"It was in a club."

"And you brought Dax with you?" he asked in surprise.

"No." Dax turned serious. "She got into a fight with a guy in the alleyway, and I pulled him off her."

Charlie didn't look surprised by the news at all. He'd heard all my stories. He took another bite.

Dax raised an eyebrow. "That doesn't concern you?"

"She's a crazy-ass bitch, man. You have no idea." He scooped his spoon into the bowl and placed it in his mouth, his eyes on the TV.

"I'll take that as a compliment." I grabbed Dax's hand and pulled him down the hallway. We went into my bedroom, and I pushed his jacket off his shoulders, watching it slide to the floor. My hands worked his tie then the buttons of his shirt.

He watched me get him naked, his eyes on me, but his usual look of desire absent.

"What?" I undid all the buttons then pushed that off his shoulders. I pulled the tie from around his neck.

He continued to stare, continued to hold his silence.

He usually spoke his mind, and when he didn't, I realized he was difficult to read. I ran the tie through my fingers. "This looks secure, right?"

His eyes immediately went to my fingers.

"Tie me to the headboard." My hand went to his slacks, and I got his belt undone, his button open. Then I pushed everything down, revealing a cock that was hard and ready to go. I returned the tie to around his neck, and I pulled him to the bed, seeing his eyes darken, the excitement tightening his features.

I lay back and raised my hands to the bars of my headboard, my dress rising up to the tops of my thighs, revealing my black thong underneath.

He stood next to the bed and stared at me, his hand automatically wrapping around his dick, his thumb swiping the drop that oozed from the tip. He was never sexier than when he was turned on, like right now, looking at me like I was the most irresistible thing on the planet.

He moved on top of me then wrapped the silk tie around my wrists before he secured them to the wooden bar. He looked at me as he did it, like he'd done this a hundred times and didn't need to watch his movements.

I leaned my head up to kiss him, feeling my thighs squeeze together because I was so anxious. I loved the scruff along his jawline, the darkness of his eyes, the way he looked dangerous and harmless at the same time.

He kissed me back, his eyes open, looking at the desire in my eyes. "Fuck..." His hand pushed up my dress and gripped my thong, and he slowly pulled it down to my thighs. He pulled away altogether to get it off my ankles. Then he wrapped the material around his dick and stroked himself for a moment before he helped himself to my nightstand, fishing out a condom and rolling it on.

I tugged on the headboard, instinctively wanting to reach for him, to pull him on top of me so he could take me to cloud nine.

He grabbed both my knees and pulled them apart, getting them wide open before he leaned down and pressed a kiss to my entrance.

I rolled my hips automatically, giving a loud moan because a simple kiss was more than enough to light me on fire. I tugged on the bars again, my thighs parting wider.

His hands scooped under my ass, and he kissed me again, his eyes on me, his tongue circling my clit before his lips sealed over me entirely and gave me a hard suck.

"God..." My head rolled back, and I looked at the ceiling, not caring if Charlie heard me. I'd heard him with girls before, and I placed a pillow over my head to silence the squeak of the bed.

Dax crawled up my body and positioned himself between my open legs, tilting his hips so the head of his dick could touch my entrance and slowly sink inside. He held his strong body on top of mine, his dark eyes looking into mine as he sank deeper and deeper.

I inhaled a deep breath, my legs starting to shake. "Dax..."

He moved all the way inside, leaving his balls against my ass. He brought his face close to mine but didn't kiss me. Then he started to thrust—hard.

"Yes..." This was exactly what I wanted, wanted it the moment I saw his gorgeous face in that stunning suit. He could fuck like other men couldn't. He could pound my pussy like he knew exactly where all my triggers were.

He did it harder and harder, breathing hard and grunting, making the headboard slam louder and louder.

I raised my head to kiss him.

He pulled away, like all he wanted to do was stare at me as he fucked me. He grabbed the top of my dress and tugged it down, making my tits pop out. "Fuck me." He clenched his jaw as he kept slamming into me, fucking me like he was really enjoying this, like this was a fantasy that really got him going. "Yes..."

HE LAY beside me with his eyes closed, his body still flushed and pumped from all the work he'd done, even though we'd finished fifteen minutes ago.

"You going to untie me?" I lay beside him, my dress to my waist, my tits out, my wrists still at the headboard.

He opened his eyes and looked at the ceiling. "No."

"It better be because you're going to fuck me. Because I ain't gonna sleep like this."

"Ain't?" He turned toward me, a slight grin on his face.

"Damn right, ain't."

"I hope you know that's not a word."

"God, please don't be the grammar police. I know how to write, and I know how to use slang, because I'm hip like that."

He reached up and tugged on the tie, making it come loose so my hands would be free.

"Thank you." I tossed the tie to the edge of the bed. I turned into him, snuggling into his side, my dress wrinkled and my heels kicked off to the edge of the bed. "You gonna sleep over?"

"No. I've got a long day tomorrow."

"Alright." I preferred not to share my bed because it was too small for a man of his size, but I'd started to get used to it, the way he sighed right when he woke up, the way he spooned me from behind or pulled me close if I was on the other side of the bed.

He turned to me and gave me a kiss before he got out of bed. He pulled on his boxers then slowly started to put each piece of his suit back on his body.

I stood up and adjusted my dress before I grabbed the tie. I caught the tag as I turned it over.

Louis Vuitton.

He had a Louis Vuitton tie?

That meant it was like three hundred dollars.

My heart started to race, finding another perplexing fact about him. Why was a man in a nearly empty apartment wearing a designer like this? He hadn't even had any suits in his closet when I was over there.

He pulled on the jacket then turned around. "Everything alright?"

I almost confronted him about it, but I didn't. I bit my tongue because Charlie would have told me to. It was a weird thing to say anyway, to question Dax about wearing something expensive. Maybe his mother gave it to him as a birthday gift or something. "Yeah." I handed over the tie.

He secured it around his neck, perfectly tying it without the need for a mirror—like he did that every single day.

I walked him to the front door. Charlie was absent from the living room, probably in the bedroom watching TV as he fell asleep.

Dax turned to me before he opened the door. "Do you have plans on Friday evening?"

"Not at the moment."

"No plans to provoke the mob or something?" he asked, slightly playful.

"Well, not right this second, but anything can happen."

"Have dinner with me. I want to talk to you about something."

"Why don't you just talk to me about it now?"

He stared at me for a while, breathing a deep sigh as he considered it. "Because it's not the right time." He leaned down and kissed me before he walked out of the apartment.

Like always, I watched him go, stared at that tight ass in those slacks.

TWENTY-FOUR
CARSON

"You wanted me, boss?" I stepped into Vince's office, staying near the door because I didn't expect this to take long.

"Clear your schedule for the day. I have another assignment for you."

I never said no to work, but I already had so much going on. I was juggling three articles at once. "What is it?"

"Vivica was supposed to interview the CEO of Clydesdale Software for an editorial piece. When we approached them about the article, they specifically asked for her."

"Then why are you making me do it?"

"Because she broke her fucking foot last night." He threw down his folder.

"What about Charlie?" If I was going to nominate someone to take over, I was going to suggest my best friend.

"He's already on assignment in Brooklyn. Look, the meeting is in thirty minutes. I just need someone to go, and you're here." He lifted the folder. "Here's all of Vivica's notes. Just make it work, alright?"

"I haven't even had time to research any of this." I walked into the office and took the folder.

"That's why I'm asking you. You're the only one who can think quickly on their feet."

I took the compliment and pulled the folder close. "Well, thank you. Why are we doing an editorial piece, though?"

"My sources tell me there's some shady stuff going on at that company. We get him on record talking about the company and whatnot, and then use that as a backdrop later."

That was brutal. "Alright. What's the guy's name?" I flipped through the paperwork but couldn't find it.

"Dax Frawley."

I slowly turned back to him, my eyebrow raised.

"What?"

"His name is Dax?"

"Yes. Why?"

It was an odd coincidence, since Dax had told me he worked at that very software company...and his name was Dax. But he never mentioned he owned the place, and that was something that would have come up by now. I'd known him for nearly five weeks at this point. Why would he lie about his job? It just didn't make sense. I wanted to jump to conclusions, but Charlie's rational voice was in my head, telling me to give Dax the benefit of the doubt.

Because I was sprung on this man.

"Carson?"

I snapped out of my thoughts. "Yeah, I'll take care of it..."

I CHECKED in at the lobby and held up my ID. "*New York Press.*"

The security officer buzzed me through. "Top floor. Check in with the assistants first."

I got into the elevator and took the long ride to the very top, nervous even though I was never nervous. I wasn't intimidated by anyone, afraid of anything. But I was afraid I'd walk into that office and see the face of the man who had been in my bed last night.

That couldn't happen.

I couldn't have two men in a row I cared about be liars.

I couldn't handle another betrayal...not when I was still hurt from the first one.

Dax wouldn't do that to me.

Right?

The doors opened, and I checked in at the front desk with a young blond woman. "Hi, I'm here for the interview with Mr. Frawley."

"Of course. Vivica?" She looked through her schedule.

"Vivica had a medical emergency, so I'm filling in."

"Alright." She nodded to the couch. "He'll be with you in a second."

I took a seat, having left the folder at home because I already knew everything I wanted to ask. I'd quickly browsed through Vivica's notes at my desk before I'd left for the interview. I had my recorder with me, hanging on the chain around my neck along with the ID card.

A minute later, the blonde walked to me, in a pencil skirt and heels. "He's ready for you."

I got up and followed her.

She led me to the double doors, both charcoal black. She held the door open for me.

"Thanks." I stepped inside the large office. There were two couches facing each other, bookshelves on either side. The desk was located on the far side of the room, in front of the floor-to-ceiling windows. I stepped inside and stared at the man leaning over his desk, his hand on the pad of his laptop as he scrolled through something at the last minute.

Brown eyes.

Dark hair.

Scruff along his jaw.

A designer suit on a chiseled body.

I stood still as I stared at him, his eyes focused on the laptop as he finished up whatever he needed to take care of before giving me his attention. My heart hadn't beat this hard in a long time, not since I'd found out my husband was a piece of shit. My eyes couldn't believe what they were seeing. Didn't want to believe what they were seeing.

I would normally scream or lose my temper, but I was quiet, speechless.

I waited for him to look at me.

He shut his laptop and straightened. "Just needed to finish something." His hands moved in his pockets as he came around the desk. He lifted his chin to address me, but instead of opening his lips to speak, he halted in place.

I stared at Dax, so livid I wasn't even sure what to say. Sometimes men took swings, and I never took it personally. Sometimes things didn't go my way, but I never got mad. But right now, I was furious...fucking furious. And I knew why.

Because I was hurt.

I was hurt for a lot of reasons. More than I could share at that moment. But the biggest hurt of all was that Dax knew I'd been hurt, betrayed, and then he did it again. He'd lied to me. Fucking lied to me.

When he recovered from the shock, he moved forward again. "Carson, let me explain—"

"You're a billionaire CEO. No explanation required." I turned away and opened the door. I left it open on purpose, so his assistants could hear the insults I unleashed. My head turned his way, and I kept my voice calm, holding the higher ground and keeping my dignity. "And a liar. A fraud. A phony. And overall, just a really shitty person."

"WHY ARE YOU BACK SO SOON?" Vince came to my desk.

"He rescheduled." I made up a lie because I didn't want to say I ditched the interview for personal reasons.

Vince nodded. "Alright. If Vivica is up for it in a few days, I'll give the article back to her."

"Yeah..."

Vince walked away.

My phone had been ringing nonstop because Dax kept calling me. I got so tired of it that I just blocked him.

Charlie walked into the office a moment later, his satchel over his shoulder. He came to my cubicle but stilled when he saw the look on my face. "Geez, what happened?"

"Why do you assume anything happened?"

"Because you look like you're about to cry." He kneeled so no one else could overhear our conversation.

I was hurt, but I wasn't going to shed a single tear over that asshole. "I don't cry, Charlie."

"What happened?" he whispered.

"Let's talk about it later."

He still looked anxious and refused to leave, like the concern was too much for him to walk away.

"Let's just say that my hunch about Dax was right."

THE SECOND we left the office, Charlie was on me. He couldn't ask me anything in the elevator because people were with us, but when we were on the sidewalk, the words launched out of his mouth. "What are you talking about?"

"I'm talking about the fact that I knew something was wrong, but you told me to deny my instincts. This is all your fucking fault, Charlie. My instincts have helped me survive, have gotten me where I am today, and I knew there was something up with that asshole, but you told me to ignore it."

"Whoa..." He raised both hands in the air, visibly offended. "Let's take it down a notch, alright?"

I immediately felt guilty, knowing Charlie just wanted the best for me, just wanted me to be happy. "I'm sorry..." I ran my fingers through my hair and stared at the sidewalk for a second. "I just... I'm fucking furious right now."

"What happened?" He came closer to me, his hands gripping my arms. "Did you see him with someone else?"

"No."

"Then what?"

"Vince made me pick up Vivica's editorial. I was supposed to interview the CEO of Clydesdale Software. Well, guess who the CEO is."

His eyebrows slowly furrowed. "Dax?"

"Yep. Fucking billionaire in a designer suit."

He dropped his hands. "So, this guy is a billionaire, and you're mad because...?"

"Because he's a liar and a damn hypocrite. He told me to lower my walls and give him a chance and all this bullshit, and he was lying about who he was the entire time. I don't even know this guy. He took me to some fake apartment where he obviously doesn't live. It's all a lie. It's all an illusion. He even asked me to be exclusive, and he still didn't tell me who he was. Who the hell does that?"

Charlie's eyes fell the longer he listened to me.

"The worst part? He knows how damaged I am from my divorce, how much that fucked me up, how hard it is for me to trust someone. And he chose to keep lying to me. He chose to mislead me. Who does that?"

He slipped his hands into his pockets and released a sigh. "Yeah...I get what you're saying."

I held up my hands. "Who is this guy? Seriously? Everything I know about him is a lie."

"Well, I doubt it's everything..."

"And I couldn't care less about him being a billionaire. That doesn't make him look better, but worse. He lied to me because I'm insignificant to him. He's got all the power and money, and I mean nothing."

"Okay, the guy is a jerk, but he's not evil. I doubt that's how he thinks."

"Whatever. I walked in there and saw him in his fancy suit in his fancy office, and he looked like a damn pussy, his eyes wide because he'd been caught. Same fucking look on his face as when I caught my husband with his pants down."

He bowed his head and shook his head slightly. "I'm sorry, Carson..."

"It's not your fault." Hearing the genuine disappointment in his voice dulled my anger, made my voice grow quiet. I crossed my arms over my chest and ignored the people passing us on the sidewalk.

"No. You recognized the signs, and I told you to ignore them. I'm sorry about that."

"You just wanted to give him the benefit of the doubt."

"Well, I was wrong, apparently."

I rubbed my arms as I felt the throbbing in my chest. "If it were some other guy, I would just shake it off. But...I really liked him. He was... It doesn't matter. I should have known he was too good to be true. Guys like that are never real. Their only purpose is to break your heart."

He came closer to me and wrapped his arms around me. "I'm sorry." He held me close and rubbed my back, his chin resting on top of my head. He gave me an affectionate squeeze, making me feel loved, making me feel like I still had a lot to be thankful for.

I sighed into his shirt, loving his support. "I'll be alright." I forced myself to pull away and put on a brave face. "I'm not gonna let a man destroy me, not again. Let's just move on."

He continued to wear that look of pity. "Carson, you're going to find the right guy... I know you will."

"Maybe. And he'll be nothing like that piece of shit Dax Frawley."

I SAT on the couch with a beer in my hand, watching the game and trying not to think about the man who'd burned me. A day had passed, and I was still furious. A good night of rest hadn't diminished the rage.

I wasn't just mad at him—but myself.

The signs were there, but I ignored them.

I let him play me for a fool.

How many other women had he done this to?

Why did he have to do it in the first place? A sexy billionaire could get laid whenever he wanted.

A loud knock sounded on the door.

Charlie turned to me. "Expecting anyone?"

I shook my head.

He walked to the door and checked the peephole. Then he turned back to me. He mouthed, "It's him."

I rolled my eyes. "Fuck off, Dax!"

He knocked again. "Open the door."

"Nope." I drank from my beer.

He knocked again, this time louder. "Sweetheart, please."

"Oh, hell no." I got off the couch and walked to the door.

Charlie immediately stepped to the side because he knew shit was about to go down.

I opened the door to him on the doorstep, in jeans and a shirt. Handsome as ever, but those qualities were replaced by an ugliness that came from deep within. "Don't ever call me that again." I splashed the beer in his face, making a mess all over his clothes. "And leave me the fuck alone." I slammed the door in his face.

Charlie stood there, eyes wide and in shock at what I'd just done.

Dax didn't give up. He knocked again.

"Just ignore him." I put the empty beer bottle on the counter.

This time, Dax just let himself inside, his face clean because he'd wiped it on the front of his shirt. "Carson, let me explain—"

"Just because you're a billionaire doesn't give you the right to barge in here." I turned to him, my hand on my hip. "Maybe we're just fucking commoners to you—"

"I just want to talk to you." He held up both hands. "Come on. Please."

Charlie started to head to the living room.

"You stay right there." I pointed at him. "Dax was just leaving." I turned back to him. "Get out of our apartment. Now."

Charlie stilled, but it was obvious he didn't want to be a part of this. He slid his hands into his sweatpants and tried to direct his stare on something other than the two of us.

"I'm not leaving." Dax stood in front of me, his clothes soaked in the beer I'd thrown at him. His hair was damp too. His eyes were intense and full of remorse, and his devastatingly good looks could persuade anyone to do anything.

"Would you like me to escort you out myself?" I asked, full of threat. "Because I can."

He didn't take that threat seriously, based on his stoic expression.

"She's not kidding, man," Charlie said. "She's taken a lot of classes…"

I stayed still and gave Dax a chance to leave on his own.

He inhaled a deep breath. "I was going to tell you on Friday."

"I don't give a shit when you were going to tell me, Dax. That's not the problem—"

"I know I shouldn't have lied at all. But it's impossible for me to meet a woman who wants me and not my money. The second they know who I am, they treat me differently. They either get greedy or weird. I just wanted to connect with someone on a real level without my wealth being a focal point."

Charlie shifted his gaze to me, slightly less angry.

"My wife only wanted me for my money, and I didn't see it. She used me, manipulated me, and I just…didn't want to go through that again. I'm not a bad guy, Carson. I just needed some privacy for a while."

Charlie watched me, empathy in his gaze.

I wasn't so sympathetic. "So, you wanted to get to know me without risking anything?"

"I…I guess."

"Well, I'm the one who risked everything by trusting someone, which is fucking hard for me. So, while you protected yourself, I put myself out there completely. How do you think that makes me feel?"

He inhaled quietly, the softness entering his eyes. "Yeah… that was an asshole thing to do."

"Yeah, it fucking was, Dax. I have no idea who you are."

"I'm the same person," he said calmly. "The only thing that's changed is the size of my wallet."

"No." I shook my head. "I don't know where you live. I don't know what your life is like. I like the version of you that I met. I highly doubt I'm going to like the billionaire playboy who's got twenty cars at his penthouse."

"I'm not a playboy—"

"How would I know?" I countered. "Because I don't know you at all."

"Then get to know me again," he said, practically pleading. "I really like you, Carson—"

"I don't like you—because I don't know you. You're literally a stranger to me."

"Come on, that's not true."

"I was in a relationship where the asshole lied to my face. You lied to me every single day."

"I didn't—"

"You took me to a fake apartment. You know how creepy that is?"

He was quiet, having no defense.

"You took me to fancy places and made me feel bad you were paying because I didn't know you could afford to buy the damn restaurant—in cash."

He bowed his head.

"I left my phone at your apartment, and you said you had gone to help a friend—which was obviously a lie."

Now, he really looked guilty.

"Lies. Lies. Lies." I held up both hands. "I'm done with lies. If I'm going to be in a relationship with someone again, it's going to be based on honesty. I can't be with someone who respects me so little."

"I do respect you—"

"People who respect you don't lie to your face. They don't ask for an exclusive relationship without giving you the full story. They don't ask to fuck you without a condom."

He kept his eyes down, full of shame.

"If we were just fucking around without an emotional attachment, I wouldn't have cared. But you're the one who wanted to step it up, to ask for more, to tell me I was the one who needed to get my shit together." I walked toward him, pointing at his face. "How dare you treat me that way and make me feel like shit when you were the one with your walls up? You're such an asshole, Dax."

He closed his eyes and sighed. "I-I didn't handle it well. I just didn't expect to like you so much. I didn't expect that this would go somewhere."

"When it did, you could have told me, and none of this would have happened."

"I know, but the longer I waited, the more afraid I became that you wouldn't forgive me."

"So, stepping into your office to interview you was the best choice?" I asked sarcastically.

"I didn't think it was going to be you—"

"I know," I snapped. "Because you specifically asked for Vivica."

He closed his eyes again.

I knew that was the final nail in his coffin.

"You asked for Vivica deliberately, to keep this lie going. And that is fucking disgusting."

He was silent.

"Get out of my apartment, Dax. And fuck off on your way out."

ALSO BY E. L. TODD

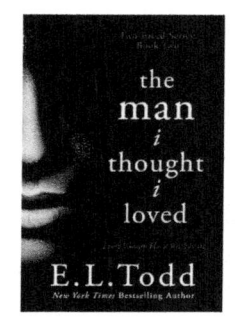

Two-Faced.

That's exactly what he is.

A liar.

I've already been ripped into a million pieces before, and I don't have the strength to do it again. Thankfully, he didn't have much of me to begin with. I was smart about it, not giving my heart away as easily as my body.

But he's still there...everywhere.

My friends tell me to forgive and forget, to give him another chance.

Sure, I can forgive.

But never forget.

Order Now

Printed in Great Britain
by Amazon